A WISH OF ASHES AND GLASS

Published by Fairies and Fantasy Pty Ltd 2023
A Wish of Ashes and Glass copyright © 2023 Selina Fenech
Cover art and interior illustrations © 2023 Selina Fenech

www.selinafenech.com

ISBN: 978-1-922390-75-2 (eBook)
ISBN: 978-1-922390-76-9 (paperback)
ISBN: 978-1-922390-77-6 (hardcover)

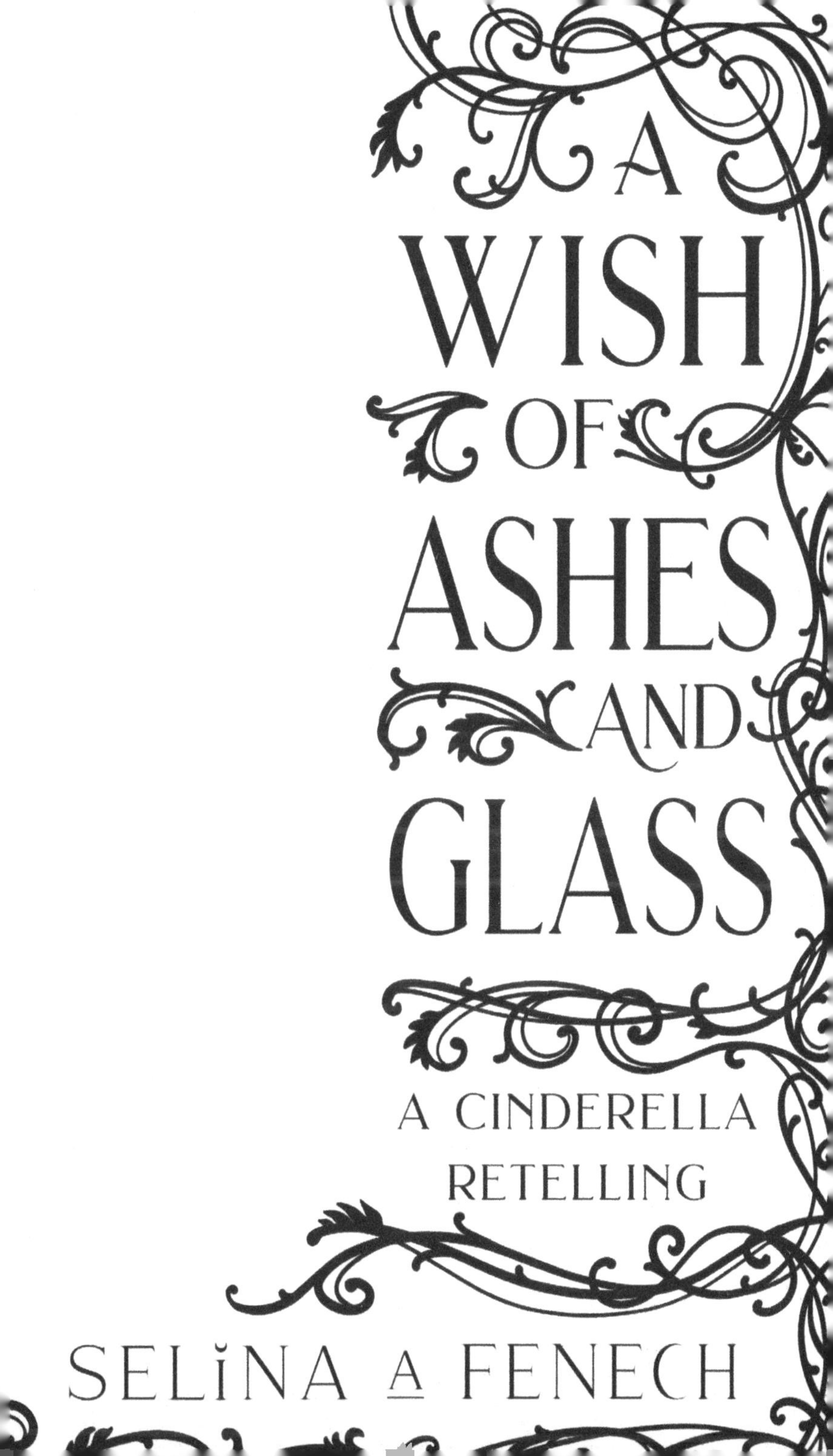

A WISH OF ASHES AND GLASS
A CINDERELLA RETELLING
SELINA A FENECH

ONE

WHAT'S ONE MORE scar when your whole life is pain?

I tallied new marks on my skin daily. A tapestry of tiny afflictions. I had taken them willingly, so I certainly wouldn't complain about their presence.

"I'm sorry I didn't get to you sooner," I whispered.

The soft glow of dawn reached delicate fingers in through gaps in the barn walls. I examined the glue trap and the mouse attached to it. All four legs and the tail were firmly stuck down. One front leg had broken in several places in the tiny animal's desperate struggles to free itself.

I murmured soft, comforting sounds as I dripped oil around the panicking animal and worked to pry it free with the edge of a spoon. "I know, I know. You poor sweet thing.

You can't understand I'm trying to help. But you will soon. Just don't break any more limbs before then, please?"

The process was tedious and just one of many. Doing the rounds checking and clearing all the traps on the property took hours each morning. *Not as though I haven't any other chores to be doing. But none are as important as this.* It simply meant I had to rise earlier each day, but this was a job best done in the dark, so nobody else knew.

The mouse whimpered a squeak as its final paw came free from the trap, and I scooped it into the palm of my hand. It lay on its side, slicked in oil, chest heaving in pained breaths.

The broken leg had ruptured like a nasty spot of dropped jam. Its other front paw was curled painfully too. A white paw, contrasting the dull gray brown of the rest of its fur.

Poor, pretty, little thing. I glared at the glue trap, cursing the existence of such a disgusting, cruel contraption. Given my way, I wouldn't have them anywhere on my family's property, but my stepfather insisted. I could hear Lord Trolaine's ranting voice in my head. He certainly wasn't going to allow vermin and pests to steal what belonged to him.

I hadn't won my plea to refuse the worst of trapping options, no matter what alternatives I offered. So instead, I tried to reduce the harm caused by them as much as I could after the fact.

My vow to always heal others—providing it didn't cost my

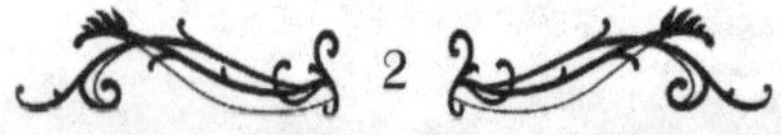

own life, I reasoned—hadn't been made excluding animals.

The mouse's wounds were grim, and I cringed at the thought of suffering those injuries myself. A broken leg would be excruciating. But the mouse was only a tiny thing, with tiny injuries, at least compared to me. They would grow no larger when they became mine—the exchange never scaled ailments up or down.

Much like the sparrow I'd found earlier, almost dead from poisoning. What was life-threatening for the small bird was now only a low churning in my stomach.

And what was a torn limb and broken fingers for a mouse would be bearable for me. I cooed a soothing sound and opened my magic to take the animal's injuries. Touch and intent were all I needed, and the mouse twitched and chirruped as its wounds closed and bones knit. An ache shot down the fingers of my hand, and on my other, the skin over a knuckle split. I sucked in a sharp breath.

Not bad, but deep enough to scar. Just one more to add to the collection already decorating my body.

The mouse's chest still puffed like the smallest of bellows, and it stared up at me with wide, black eyes.

"Feeling better?"

It twitched its nose and tentatively rolled onto all fours. Then it leapt off and disappeared, quiet as a shadow, behind the hay bales.

"I'll take that as a yes," I whispered.

Recorking the small oil bottle, I put it and the spoon back in my pocket. I scooped a small handful of old chaff from the floor and sprinkled it over the trap as though some animal had kicked it on there. That would disguise the mess the oil had left. It would also help stop any other creatures getting stuck for now. Still, Trolaine would replace the trap with a new one soon, and I'll be back here, repeating the process.

Wincing as I stood back up, I brushed down my stained apron. That was the last trap until tomorrow. I would remove them entirely if I could, but I knew Lord Trolaine did occasionally check on them himself to confirm there were no miniscule bandits pilfering his goods.

If he looked harder, he'd see they weren't. I inspected the hardwood barrels lined up along the side of the barn, in which I stored animal feed and anything else rodents might get into. The hours I spent last autumn picking and preserving pears to trade with the vintner over the hill for the old casks were well spent. Still no holes.

There were always ways to protect oneself without resorting to cruelty.

I collected a bucket and marched off to feed the ducks. Then the rest of the animals. Then milk the goats, then make bread, then hang laundry, then serve breakfast, and then, and then, and then.

A WISH OF ASHES AND GLASS

There was always so much to do, which was to be expected when I was the only person tasked with keeping the manor and fields in order. Hiring more servants would be at the expense of growing Trolaine's daughter's dowries, after all, and he would never jeopardize that.

A tugging ache had built in my lower back by the time I was preparing for breakfast. It twinged sharply as I threw the tablecloth out across the table, and I had to still for a moment until the pang passed.

Was that a pain formed on its own, or something I had taken from a creature that morning? I had healed so many, I already couldn't remember. Not that it mattered. I knew pain far more intimately than I did the lack of it, and recent years had taught me what I could endure. I'm stronger than I ever believed I could be, and in my heart I know that strength is born from kindness.

My younger stepsister yawned her way into the room and dumped herself into a chair. Her doll-like freckled face was drawn downward in its usual dejected expression, which only lifted into a forced smile at times when her father was present.

I fetched the kettle from the hearth and brought it to the table to fill the teapot. "Up late reading again?"

Asterra's lips pursed. "How do you know these things? Do you spy on me at night, Cinders?"

I bit my lip, my eyes drawn to the prominent burn scars

on my hands and forearms. The three of us stepsisters all had nicknames for each other, ones created playfully during adventurous games imagining ourselves as lady pirates on the high seas when we were young. But a subtle cruelty had crept into those names the older we got.

The reddened wrinkles were the result of an act I was proud of, but in a household where a young woman's only value was her perfect appearance—for how else would she be perfectly marriageable?—that was a hard pride to hold on to.

"Terra, do you really think I have the time or inclination to spy on you? Perhaps I had some other clues." I smirked and pointed. "Like the lamp soot on your fingers or the lilac under your eyes." *And a long history of being scolded about the habit by a father more interested in making sure his daughter remained more pretty than educated.*

Asterra's face moved slowly, sleepily into a wide-eyed expression of realization, and she began scrubbing her fingertips with the hem of the tablecloth.

"Little Terra, you really are an open book." Audred, the eldest stepsister, swept into the room with a swish of skirts, her strawberry-blond ringlets hanging loose around her petite face. Her every movement was precise and ladylike as she bent to kiss her sister good morning. "And Father will punish you worse for staining the linens than he will for not getting your beauty sleep."

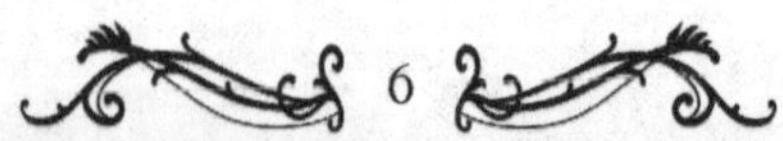

A WISH OF ASHES AND GLASS

Terra and Dred—a perfect pair, with matching peach-toned hair and a blush of starry freckles across sharp cheekbones. They could almost be twins, but the three of us never passed as blood sisters.

My pale, mousy-blond tresses were kept bundled out of the way under a fraying scarf, and my skin, where unmarred by scarring, was a sickly milky tone, smudged in dirt, bruises, and ash. They were all glowing golden sunset, and I was a washed-out winter sky, grayed by a coming storm.

Audred assessed the table spread and tsked. "You're behind, Cinders. Father will be here soon." She plucked the stack of plates from my hands, and I nodded a mute thank you. Any gratitude greater than that only made things awkward in our already fraught relationship.

She gave a wry smile in return and shooed me toward the kitchen before turning to lay out the plates. "Oh! This teapot always reminds me of the play one we had when we were young. Do you remember it? We'd fill it with water and mint leaves and set it in the sun."

Although my stepsisters and I shared no blood, there were some fond memories between us, back in the time when we played together freely and felt like a family. Before death and my stepfather's machinations interrupted our youth and drove a wedge between the daughters of his blood, and those not.

I smiled wanly at Audred as I returned with a tray of

bread and jams. "It's been a long time since we held tea parties, not since …"

Audred laid out the final plate, hand lingering on it as she held my gaze, her practiced, doe-eyed, sweet expression slipping into something pained and real.

"Audred, what on earth are you doing?" Lord Trolaine stood at the doorway, glaring at the plate under Audred's fingertips. Tall and lean, he loomed over the three of us like a specter, grumbling around his bushy red moustache.

Audred jumped about a foot, spun on the spot, neatened her dress, and fixed her face into the expression she presented to her father when he most required placating.

"Act like a servant, and a servant's lot is all you'll deserve." Trolaine flicked an invisible speck from his suit as he strolled to the head of the table in long strides.

"I was only … Cind … Ellasyn was making a mess of the setting, so I was straightening it out." Her eyes avoided mine as she took a seat after him and folded her hands in front of her, neat and still. I continued with the breakfast service, unfazed, as being thrown under the carriage by my stepsisters wasn't new to me.

Asterra shifted from drowsy slump to propped-up puppet. A straight smile tensed her lips as she cast concerned glances between us all.

"Then you reprimand the servant, not assist her. Otherwise,

how is she to ever learn?" Trolaine flicked out his napkin and lay it on his lap, speaking as though I was not even in the room. "Girls, do you wish to be commoners, or do you wish to be treated as royalty?"

"Royalty, Father," Audred and Asterra chimed together.

"Would royalty set their own table?"

"No, Father."

"Then behave like royalty." Trolaine snapped a finger at Audred.

Cheeks flushing beneath her freckles, she drew herself up and glared at me. "This breakfast has been slovenly and slow. Our settings are crooked, our tea not yet poured, our food not yet served, and … and this tablecloth is marked with soot. You must learn to do better, or you will be cast out and replaced."

The threat was empty. Trolaine would then have to pay someone, or multiple servants, for all the work he didn't pay me for. Still, I hung my head, suitably repentant, to avoid threats of punishment that weren't empty.

"And what penalty does our servant deserve from such failure? How many strikes of the cane?"

Threats like that one. My skin chilled.

Audred's eyes flickered past mine and her eyelashes fluttered. "T … T—"

Trolaine shook his head.

"Th—"

He nodded approvingly.

"Three strikes of the cane," Audred proclaimed firmly, then looked at her plate. A shiver rippled over her shoulders.

"Very good. Ellasyn, come to my chambers after breakfast. I will see to your punishment so you will learn to remain respectful and productive."

I stared, unblinking for a long moment, fury rising within me. Fury at this man who has taken so much from me with no regard for anything but his own selfish wishes.

It was times like this when I considered simply leaving. But I could imagine living destitute on the streets would also have its cruelties. At least here, they were a known quantity. At least here, I was in my family home, even if it no longer belonged to me. It was all I had left. And I knew what I could endure.

"Yes, my lord. I will strive to do better." I schooled my face, dipped a curtsey, and served breakfast. Pain, I could suffer. Loss, I could not.

"You are both looking lovely this morning," Trolaine told his daughters as he spread jam onto a thick crust. "Asterra, lift your posture. Audred, decent women do not wear their hair loose in public. Please be sure to have it done before breakfast in the future."

"Yes, Father."

A WISH OF ASHES AND GLASS

"Thank you, Father."

They both adjusted themselves, smiled prettily, and nodded.

I brought out a second tray of cheese and fruit, trying to focus only on the next task at hand and not the unfair punishment awaiting me afterward. The freshly made cheese smelled milky and sweet, and my stomach rumbled.

But I would not be eating with them. Lord Trolaine was quite specific on the amount of food I prepared each day and made sure what he allotted served only three. I would make do with leftovers and yesterday's stale bread once their breakfast was done.

Trolaine lifted his teacup for a refill, sneering at me as I hurried to his side, before turning his attention back to his daughters. "After all my hard work to build your dowries"—I tensed, almost spilling the tea. All the wealth accrued in this family had come from my mother. Apparently, marrying rich counted as hard work. As Lord Trolaine was the only one who had done so, I'd have to take his word for it—"we've started attracting the interest of some fine suitors recently, including a few barons. Although I still hope for a grander match. A count, or perhaps a duke, would be more deserving of my precious daughters."

Audred's hand fluttered to her chest. "A duke? I could truly be worth such an arrangement?"

"Why stop there? The crown prince still isn't married,"

Asterra said before covering her smile with a sip of tea. I was glad for her that her mocking tone seemed completely lost on the rest of her family.

Audred gasped in enthusiastic ignorance. "Oh, do you think I'm beautiful enough for Prince Creston?"

"More than, my dearest," Trolaine replied.

"*Dearest?*" Asterra plunked down her teacup, apparently aghast her joke turned against her. "What about me? Aren't I worthy of a prince?"

"Not with those tired eyes," Audred muttered.

Asterra grunted and opened her mouth wide to retort, but Trolaine slapped his hand down on the table. My heart raced at the sound, knowing the smack of the cane would be much the same, thanks to all the times I had heard it before. Asterra and Audred stilled. They were familiar with the sound too.

"Behavior, girls! Squabbling is unattractive. More's the shame there aren't two princes so you could have one each as you deserve. But you will only earn such an offer if you control yourselves and your emotions."

"Yes, Father," they said together and returned quietly to their food.

Some days, I pitied them as I would livestock whose only fate was to be fattened for auction. But there was little use in pity from someone already a commodity under another's control, one who hadn't even been worth selling.

A WISH OF ASHES AND GLASS

THE BACKS OF my legs stung fiercely as I weaved my way down to the furthest field at the bottom of the property, further than my stepfamily ever ventured. Terra and Dred considered anything beyond the courtyard too rural and filthy for their elegant feet to tread. Trolaine kept away from the orchard and the graveyard that lay within as though it held ghosts he couldn't face.

Stepping under the cover of the ancient orchard, I breathed deep of the orange blossom fragrance that thickened the air. The fruit trees formed a thick grove around the family burial ground, and I ran my fingertips over the mossy headstones. "Morning, Grandmamma. Morning, Pa." I wished I had more time to spend on the upkeep of the graves, but I had enough to do keeping clean the areas Lord Trolaine's gaze did fall upon.

Considering what had become of my mother's grave, I was happy Lord Trolaine never saw this miraculous place. The last time any of them had visited was the day my mother was buried, as though she never existed, and never meant anything to them at all.

"Morning, Mamma."

The soft *tick, tick, tick* of the clock came as a reply. I craned

my neck, staring up into the dappled light that streamed through the trinket-encrusted hazel tree.

Colored feathers, polished pebbles, scraps of bright ribbon, shiny buttons, dinted cogs, shells from a distant sea I could only dream of, pretty pieces of broken porcelain, and a million other worthless treasures enameled the twisted trunk and hung like chimes from the branches.

Within the largest fork of the tree, somehow, miraculously, the items had formed together into a working clock, that whirred and tocked as mismatched hands kept the time, powered by some unexplainable magic of its own.

The hem of my skirt tugged, and I glanced down. A mouse with one white paw clawed at the stained fabric. It held a short piece of copper wire in its mouth.

"Hello again. Did you bring a gift for my tree?" I knelt and placed my hand flat in front of the mouse. It didn't hesitate to step onto my palm, and I stood again. "It's lovely. Thank you. Would you find a place for it for me?"

I reached up, lifting the mouse to a branch. It skittered off my hand, creeping along a surface more trinket than tree. For some reason that made sense in its mousy brain, it chose a place for the wire and wove it into the treasure tree. The branch twisted and shimmered, humming with magic as that piece became part of the whole.

Magic wasn't unheard of in Estoria, and magic had been

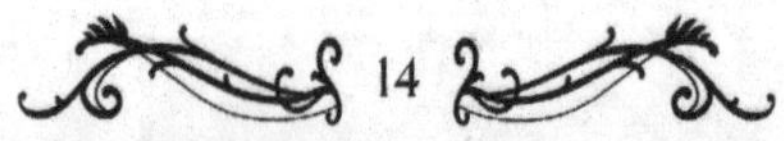

present for a few generations in my family, but I could never understand how the animals who brought me gifts knew where to place them to keep growing my tree of treasures. I liked to believe it was Mamma who spoke to them and told them where to put each new trinket. And every tiny act of gratitude had grown together into a glorious vision.

I had so few memories of my father I could count them on my scarred fingers. But my mother's death, the memories of our time together and her love now lost, was still so fresh and a pervasive, overwhelming pain. More painful than any injury I had endured since.

We had been so happy together, just she and I. Even after she had remarried and Lord Trolaine, Audred, and Asterra came to join us at the family home, we had been happy. Mamma spread happiness like dandelion seeds in the wind, and it blossomed everywhere she went. Trolaine never doted on me as much as his daughters, but he hadn't been cruel in those early days.

Then it all ended with a riding accident. Mamma refused to let me help, refused to let me take her injuries, and she died. Every day, I regret listening to her wishes, and it breaks me to know I could have saved her, but I didn't.

Never again. Never will I watch uselessly as someone or something suffers again. Not if I can endure the pain instead.

Everything changed with her death. Lord Trolaine's

priorities became ruthlessly clear, and I also lost a father and my sisters. I often wondered whether the pain I could have taken from Mamma then would have been more than what I felt at her absence now.

If she had been trying to save me from suffering, it was a flawed attempt. I hurt so much I wanted to throw myself on the grave and spend the whole day weeping. But the clock buzzed and ticked, reminding me of the hour. I can't change the past, and there was too much work to be done to waste time feeling sorry for myself.

I was trudging back through the tiered fields when Audred's overexcited voice pierced the air. "Cinders! Come quick! We have to go into town right *now*!"

TWO

IT HAD BEEN a warm, dry spring, and a hot wind gusted along the main street of Estoria, buffeting around swirls of dust and the squealing children who played in it. From our high vantage point—the balcony of one of Trolaine's acquaintance's apartments he'd somehow invited himself and us into—I looked over the chaos below.

We clearly weren't alone in having heard the gossip that some of the royal family would be passing through sometime that day. The streets were packed, as though an impromptu festival had been set up that morning, filled with many young women and men hoping for a glimpse of the heirs.

Asterra had rattled out a long list of names I was sure to instantly forget: "King Othon, Princesses Diony, Cara,

Mayree, Miara, Millette, Ava, Neeva, Lienne, Shontessa, Brialla, Mirrelle, and Elsbeth. And *of course*, Prince Creston!"

All in attendance wore their finest and engaged in a polite game of wrestling for frontmost positions, jostling for the best vantage point. Treat vendors had appeared to exploit the crowd and their tense anticipation with sugary distractions.

Children gathered in boisterous gangs, more interested in their rough-and-tumble games together than whatever the grown-ups were waiting for. They zoomed and dashed in and out of the crowds between bustled skirts and coattails. I watched, nostalgic of that age when I had such freedom. An age when I was happy and had the unconditional love of my sisters.

"Ellasyn, my hair!" Audred shrieked. "The wind is ruining it!"

Pulling hairpins and a comb from my pocket, I worked at tucking the larger flyaways back into Audred's ornate braids. "It's all right. Even if we see the prince—"

"He must be coming through soon. Do you think he'll wave?"

"—and even if the prince sees you—"

"We have such a lucky position thanks to Father. The prince *must* notice me."

"—he won't see a few individual hairs out of place."

"*You* would never understand!" Audred grunted. "I must be perfect. This may be my one chance!"

A WISH OF ASHES AND GLASS

"What are you doing to upset my daughter?" Trolaine turned from where he'd been deep in discussion with his gaunt-faced colleague. His cheeks turned as red as his moustache as he muttered apologies to the other man at my behavior.

Both Audred and I froze, mouths clamped shut. I risked a glimpse at her to see what guilt she may lay on me this time.

We were both spared by Asterra leaning out over the balcony and crying, "Something's happening! Someone's coming!"

My stepfamily moved quickly into position, as prominent along the balcony edge as possible without standing right up on the balustrade and holding up "Look over here!" placards. I stepped backward. I wasn't particularly keen for the royal family to see me, and drawing any attention to myself would just give Trolaine another reason to punish me.

While Audred and Asterra wore eye-catching and expensive gowns better suited for a grand ball than a day in town, I wore the same as I always wore—a tattered and stained servant uniform as gray from ashes as from the dull dye that originally colored it.

Even Trolaine had looked at me on the carriage ride in, muttering in disgust about what an embarrassment I was. But as he'd not seen it worth buying me any new clothes or allowing me the materials to make my own, I had nothing else.

So, I stayed toward the back, but curiosity drew my eyes down to the street.

The crowds surged forward for a closer look, then pushed back to make way from the main road in a sea-like swell of people as the horse hooves beat closer. Loud murmuring rippled along the street and necks craned.

A party of eleven riders came into view, organized in two neat lines of five with a leader at the front. All were dressed in worn soldier's uniforms and their horses trotted purposefully and without fanfare, parting the crowd as they went.

The wind whipped up, tossing the crowd's clothing, bonnets, and ribbons, and a tumble of black hair blew out behind the leader of the procession, drawing my attention.

It was such long hair, glossy in the sunlight. I didn't get out much, but it seemed odd for a soldier. As my eyes focused on the leader's face, the sweeping, dark eyes, the upper lip that curved out, plump as a cherry. The rider was … a woman? Was that odd too?

All my worldly knowledge was defined by best housekeeping practices, so I had little reference to draw on as to women in military positions. But whether it was an oddity or not, she was fascinating. Not much could be told about her body, as the armor she wore was identical to that of the soldiers riding in line behind her. Arms as thick, shoulders as wide.

She must be very tall. I couldn't take my eyes off her.

But within moments, she and her troop were gone, winding around a corner along the path to the palace.

A WISH OF ASHES AND GLASS

"Is that it?" Asterra whined. She leaned out dangerously over the balcony, belly resting on the balustrade and feet swinging off the floor, peering down the street.

Audred grabbed the back of her dress and pulled her in, but her eyes were also on the scene below. "Where's the prince? He must be coming through. Oh, Father, you said he would be!" Red blush spread up her neck and over her cheeks as she stamped a foot.

As though the lack of royal presence was somehow my fault, Trolaine turned on me. "You, go down and see if you can find out news of the prince's approach."

I bobbed a curtsey, then left down the stairs, grateful to have been sent off on my own but unsure as to how I was supposed to whisk up some knowledge on the royal heir's whereabouts. I decided to simply make my way down the street in the direction the group with the striking leader had come from and hope to spot some more fanfare.

Pushing my way through the crowd, I received a range of sneers and aghast glances. A man made an obvious show of dusting down his sleeve where I brushed against him, turning his nose up in disgust.

Lord Trolaine had spread rumors that I had gone quite mad after the death of my parents. That he did his best by me, but only so much could be done. That I chose to look the way I did. Explaining away the real reason for my condition, so as no one would suspect his mistreatment of me. Instead, I'd heard whispers that praised him for his kindness in putting up with me. The filthy little mad woman.

But more than filthy, I felt tired. I couldn't imagine having the energy to spare to chase after romance. Although I knew this game of prince hunting had little to do with romance, I felt Audred believed such an arranged marriage would bring her a fairytale love and a happily ever after.

I only hoped whatever man she was sold to wouldn't crush that dream too badly. Even if she no longer cared for me, I still thought of her as a sister.

Honestly, I didn't at all mind the work I did. I enjoyed keeping my family household well kept. It was the treatment I received from my stepfamily in return that cut me. I didn't just want a house. I wanted a home.

Muttering apologies as I passed, I managed to weave my way through to the front of the street, jostled by playing children who clapped and sang out the rhyming rules of their game.

Their voices were collectively loud, I almost didn't hear the horses over them. Shorter than many in the crowd, I couldn't see what approached but heard the roll and rattle of a carriage and the clatter of hooves on cobblestones, approaching fast. I turned to find my way back and report the news to my stepfamily.

A Wish of Ashes and Glass

"Watch out! Watch out!" a woman cried from nearby.

The masses of people split just in time as a procession of mounted soldiers galloped through, followed by a speeding carriage.

There were no flags or trumpets, no open windows or waving hands. Only travel at a pace unsafe and uncaring for anyone around it. I gasped as a horse hoof stomped by almost close enough to crush my toes and had to lean back to avoid being caught up in the row of stallions drawing the carriage.

A giggle twisted into a shriek as a small form bumped past me. A girl no older than five fell onto the road in front of me, rolling under the wheels. Screams arose around us as the carriage lifted and bumped right over the child.

The warmth drained from my skin and rushed into my chest, flaring my heart up like bellows on a forge. My pulse raced and my fingers trembled as I crouched beside the girl, fearful of what I would see.

The girl moved with the same wide-eyed, chest-heaving sobs I was so familiar with from the animals I saved. She pressed her hands to the ground as she attempted to right herself, to sit up, but squealed and whimpered when she tried to move her crushed leg.

"Hush, hush, it's not so bad as it seems. You'll be up and running and playing again soon," I told her, smiling gently and willing her to focus on me.

I checked the injury with my hands, feeling how the slim bone of her thigh was no longer solid. She would never run again, never play again, if something wasn't done.

I had made my vow to help others, but I had also made my promise to Mamma before she died that my magic would remain my secret. Could it be kept secret here, in a sea of spectators?

A woman behind me seemed to have fainted, causing her own circle of fuss. Most onlookers' attention turned there, unable to see the smaller tragedy lying in the dusty street, hidden under my crouching form and filthy skirts.

Up ahead, the carriage had found its way to a stop, the driver and nearby soldiers calling and arguing words muffled by the gossiping crowd.

If I were to do something, it would have to be fast. I bent low, as close to the child as I could, hiding her and my actions in the ruse of a comforting embrace. Then, with touch and intent, I opened my magic.

The girl squirmed in my arms, muffled sobs easing into hiccupping gasps.

"See? It was nothing. You're going to be fine." I choked on the words, bile rising in my throat as the pain hit me. *Please don't break. Please don't break.*

The child was much smaller than me, and I had tried to calculate and anticipate the scale of her injury on my body, holding on to the wish that it would be something I could endure, something that wouldn't cripple me permanently. But I hadn't taken a wound from another human for a long time.

The flesh of my thigh felt as though it was both crushed and seared on hot iron simultaneously. I clenched my teeth, biting off a cry that clawed at my throat. Tears streamed down my cheeks, and the girl stared up at me, her eyes wondering and fearful at my behavior.

"Jemmalyn? Jem!" A woman in a baker's uniform pushed through the crowd nearby, and the child scampered to her feet and rushed to her.

Down the street, the back window of the carriage slid open, silhouettes moving inside. This caused a mass of squeals and gasps and a stampede toward the open window. The mounted guards pushed the people back, and with a loudly barked order, the carriage began moving again.

My head scarf had fallen free, and my dirty hair came lose, hanging around my face. I wore it like a disguise, keeping me hidden from any onlookers, as I turned away. With the carriage already moving again, I wouldn't reach my stepfamily before it passed them.

They would be angry I'd failed to warn them, but I couldn't avoid that now. Better to avoid any chance of being questioned for what I'd done. My first steps were tentative, testing my weight on my aching leg. But it held, the bone bruised, possibly cracked, but not completely broken.

The pain, though, I worried it would make me crumble. I hadn't known anguish like this for a long time. Not from healing animals. Not from Trolaine's canings.

It's only pain. You can endure pain. I limped and hobbled through the crowd, who took little notice of me with the drama of the speeding procession still top of mind. But I worried I had taken on too large of an injury, risked too much for the child. What if the wound turned bad?

Leaning on a wall to catch my breath, I looked back. Through the crowd, I caught glimpses of the child and her mother. The woman chided and fussed and hugged the dusty girl, who in return told a big-mouthed, wide-eyed, arm-waving tale. The mother shook her head at what must have sounded like a wild story of make-believe and hugged her child tightly again.

I half smiled, tasting the tears that still flowed to my lips. This pain was worth it. I could tell that child was cared for, was loved. To deliver her unharmed back to her mother's arms, it was worth it.

I turned down the side street, beginning my limping march on what would be a long and sore journey home. My tears continued to fall. Not due to the pain. Because the only thing that stung more than the obtained injury was that on my return home, I would find no one to care for or love me.

THREE

THE WAY AUDRED spent the following week lamenting the swift passage of the royal carriage robbing her of her prince-spotting opportunity, one would have thought she was the one suffering the painful injury and not me.

My thigh was still stiff and sore, mottled all over with deep mulberry bruises and yellowed flesh. I bound it in bandages and applied a poultice, but it still troubled me so that I couldn't keep it a secret.

I made up a story for Trolaine that I had stumbled and fallen down some stairs and came directly home, as I was confused from bumping my head. It didn't save me from punishment for abandoning them without having given them advance notice of the carriage's approach. ("And my hair, Cinders, my *hair*!")

Audred still roamed the halls like a mournful ghost, wilting against walls with pitiful moans of how she should never have such an opportunity again. It was true that the king and his heirs rarely left the palace. Which was what made the royal family's travel the week before such a gossip-worthy event.

But I could hardly see how, even under the best conditions, Audred and the prince would have landed upon the right circumstances to fall instantly in love on that day. Even Asterra had tried to enlighten her sister with this fact, which only made Audred wail louder.

I kept my head down and focused on work, made slower by my throbbing thigh. It was also my sluggish, limping gait that allowed Asterra to reach the door before me when the bell rung just after midday. She rushed back into the kitchen, face flushed and eyes sparkling, clutching a parchment to her chest.

Audred picked dully at the remains of her lunch, long after her father and sister had left the table, and I waited patiently so I could finish clearing up when she finally decided she was done.

Spotting her sister, she grunted, "Father will skin you if you open mail meant for him."

Asterra moved close, her whisper conspiratorial. "It's not for him! It's addressed to the ladies of the household, and messengers were delivering them to every estate I could see." Her fingers worked at the seal.

Audred shot out of her chair and snatched the letter neatly into her own hands. With a tearing crack, she had it open, and her eyes widened as they skimmed the unfolded sheet.

"The king is holding a formal ball. At the palace. All unmarried women from eighteen to twenty-five years are expected to attend." Her voice grew breathier and higher by octaves as she delivered snippets of information. "To find a partner for his son!"

"*All* unmarried women?" Asterra's lips were puckered and sour at having lost claim of the parchment. "Even servants? Even beggars, or whores? Even Cinders?"

"Quite the list you've placed me at the end of there, Terra."

"Mind your manners, Terra! I'm sure it doesn't truly mean *all* women … although it does say … What do you think it means by 'expected'?" Audred's eyes flicked right and left as she read over the message again and again.

Could this invitation actually include me? Even if it did, I had no desire for romance with a prince, and while marriage to one even without romance may have more benefits than ills, I did not deceive myself into thinking a prince would ever pluck me from a crowd—of what, hundreds? Thousands?—of competing women and marry me into a life of luxury.

So, what good to me was this invitation?

Having apparently reached the same conclusion, Audred sighed greatly and threw her hands in the air, still clutching the invitation tightly. "What does it matter anyway? This isn't about *Cinders*." Bringing her hands to her chest, she stared wide-eyed at the ceiling as though a glowing faery blessing was being bestowed upon her. "This is about my second chance to win the prince's favor and hand!"

"Not *our* chance, Dred sister?"

Audred flippantly flapped a hand. "Of course. May the fairest win, and all that. At least the loser shall still have a night of dancing and fine foods. Oh, can you imagine what desserts they may have?"

My jaw slackened, and I licked my lips. Desserts? It had been years since anything sweeter than browned pieces of leftover apple had met my tongue.

And dancing? Of course there would be dancing. How long had it been since I danced? How long had it been since my body was used for anything other than menial labor? How long since I had free time that was more than short moments of sleep when I was too exhausted to even appreciate the rest?

A strange, tugging, hollow sensation built under my ribcage. I ... wanted to go. I *yearned* to go. Who cared about princes when there was dancing and desserts to be had?

"Keep your mind on those sweets, because you'll be stuffing your face with them as I dance all night with the prince," Asterra snapped, trying to snatch the invitation.

Audred danced the parchment out of reach and, with a wicked smile, opened her mouth. *"FATHER!"*

Her cry pierced the house, echoing around the walls, and Lord Trolaine soon stomped in.

"It is the height of vulgarity to raise your voice so. What is the matter, girl?"

Audred fluttered to his side, displaying the invitation under his nose.

"Asterra opened this." She shot a sly smile back at her pouting sister. "But look! Oh, Father, look!"

It only took a moment of stern reading before he muttered, "You'll both need new dresses. The date is but a week away. We must act swiftly. Every dressmaker will be overrun."

Audred gasped dramatically. "You're so clever. I wouldn't have thought!" Her eyes swiveled, more thoughts clearly working through her mind, then her gaze landed on me in a rare expression of sympathy. "Two dresses, though? Only, the wording of the invitation, I mean. I wasn't sure."

Trolaine looked from me to the invitation again. "But that's ridiculous. They don't truly expect it."

"But if they did truly expect all women noted to attend," I offered with my eyes lowered, hoping the yearning that had grown inside me wasn't obvious on the outside, "it would be best that we follow royal decree, would it not? There would be some who know of my belonging to this household, and if it was found out I didn't attend, that disobedience may seem an insult to the royal family."

"As though your attendance would be missed," Trolaine scoffed. "Still, that can be seen both ways. I'm sure you would be just as invisible at such a grand event, and certainly no competition for the prince's attention. Not scarred to ugliness as you are."

The gushing enthusiasm in the room ebbed, both Audred and Asterra growing quiet. They would call me Cinders every day, but never had they called me ugly due to my scars. But the pity I saw in their expressions then was as blunt a force as their father's words.

Was I ugly? It had been so long since I was even completely clean that I wasn't sure what I looked like underneath all the dirt and grime. And I didn't care. Dancing and desserts didn't care if I was ugly. I nodded my head once.

"I'm sure you're right, Lord Trolaine. I only wish to meet the requirements of the invitation and would never be competition to your daughters."

He stared at me for a long moment, a judging twinkle in his eye. "An arrangement may be made, then. You've been far too lazy recently. Pretending to limp about the house, no doubt attempting to seek sympathy for your last caning. Perhaps we can use the treat of the ball as motivation for you.

A WISH OF ASHES AND GLASS

You can go if all your chores are completed in time. All your normal duties, whatever it is that you waste so many hours on each day, and I'll also provide a proper list of tasks to make sure you're spending your time productively."

Wonderful. I could only imagine what he presumed would be better ways to handle the housekeeping. Perhaps I should never have opened my mouth. But desserts … I hoped signing up for this extra work would be worth it. "Very well, my lord."

Audred and Asterra remained impassive, as though unsure whether they wanted me to attend along with them. They never used to worry about being seen with me in public, but it seems that may have changed with this invitation.

"Girls, prepare quickly. We must hurry to arrange your gowns." Turning on his heel, Trolaine marched to the door. He paused in the threshold and called back at me, "Oh, and I shan't buy you a dress.

THE TIPS OF my fingers were scraped raw by the night of the ball, and my tired eyes felt just as red. The burn scars on my hands felt tight and painful from overuse. My hours working every day through Trolaine's list were long, added to by staying up late trying to stitch together some semblance of a respectable dress from old, unused curtains.

Audred fretted incessantly right up to the moment it was time to leave.

She spoke an endless stream of nerves as I helped her with her hair and gown. "I suppose, even if we don't catch the prince's eye, there must be other nobility in attendance. Even if we can't assume the highest catch, we can at least hope to attract the interest of another match that would honor our family. But we must also strive for the very best. It would be cowardly and slothful not to. Dare I hope? Yet there will be simply so many women in competition. Is my gown suitable? Perhaps red was not the right color choice after all. It had seemed so striking, but surely that would be a common thought and I will be lost now in a sea of red! I must be cleverer tonight. I must be my most beautiful. It's just too important of an opportunity, no matter how one looks at it. We cannot be anything less than perfect. Oh, these shoes look so clunky."

Asterra had matched her sister's nervous energy with a silent tension. Then the carriage arrived, and they and their father left without me. For of course I wasn't ready to leave, nor had I completed Trolaine's impossibly long list of chores.

"You'll have to find your own way," was all I was told as their carriage drove off.

I battled through the last three items on Trolaine's awful list—polish the silver that was never used, scrub the ceiling

in the parlor (the ceiling!), and restack the firewood "in a more eye-pleasing manner"—through sheer stubbornness, all the while not seeing a solution as to how I would find my way to the ball, only that it was my end goal.

Finish the work, finish the dress, and then perhaps find a sense of peace and joy for a few short hours in dancing and delicious treats. I would walk there if I had to. It would take me what, two hours, maybe three? Less if I took a shortcut through the woods. Would that be safe?

Of course, I would also need a finished dress. It was still so far from done, but if I danced in the shadows, no one would see the raw ends of the fabric and missing trim. And if I put my hair in a tight bun, no one needed to know it had not been washed. If I sewed on buttons rather than lacing, it would at least fit functionally and be done faster. And I knew I had plenty of buttons to use.

By lamp light, I made my way down the trail through the fields to the orchard. When had it gotten so dark? My leg no longer ached recklessly, but I still moved hesitantly on it, especially with exhaustion making my steps wobbly on uneven ground.

Blearily, I blinked at my treasure tree, holding the lamp up to search for buttons that would match the others I had already sewn to the dress. The clock reflected down at me, round and bright as a full moon, both hands pointing mostly upward.

No. No it can't be. When was the last time I'd seen the time? How had so many hours passed? The ball must be nearly over and surely would be by the time I found my way there.

I had missed out.

It was hopeless, and I was a fool for ever having hoped in the first place.

A wracking, coughing sob shot through me, and I crumpled at the foot of the tree. One of my hands reached out desperately and wrapped around the headstone of Mamma's grave, clinging for support.

There was no comfort in that cold, weathered stone. It held neither the warmth nor the softness of my mother's loving embrace, that I would never feel again. That I longed for so dearly.

It wasn't *fair.* I had worked so hard and hadn't asked for anything in return. Not a dress, not to ride in the carriage, nothing more than to use a few hours of my own time in a way I might enjoy, and I couldn't even have that.

It was obvious Trolaine had never intended me to reach the ball. Had thwarted my attempt with ridiculous chore lists and expectations. And if I complained? If I made a sound at the cruelty of denying me that small freedom, I knew I would be blamed. He would find great joy in pointing out that my inability to go to the ball was, by his technicalities, my own fault.

A WISH OF ASHES AND GLASS

How long could I keep living like this? What sort of life was this?

My tears dripped from my cheeks, soaking into the ground, and the clock made a strange clang. I looked up, expecting to hear it chime midnight.

Instead, the whole tree shimmered and trembled.

Trinket-laden branches jingled. A soft glow grew on the clockface and spread down the trunk of the tree. There was movement around me too, small forms skittering in the dark. Little mice, rabbits, sparrows, rats, bats, squirrels, hedgehogs—all the creatures I had rescued from Trolaine's traps. Never had I seen so many together at once.

The treasure tree shivered again, metal and porcelain trinkets singing like windchimes in the quiet night, and then a louder, tearing crackling followed. I feared the slim tree would break apart and fall. A star-bright line traced down the trunk from the clock to the ground, then the tree split down the middle.

The line widened, opening into an arching doorway that sparkled and shimmered within, filled with a liquid, mirror-like surface. I saw myself in that watery mirror, broken, yet with a strong resolve on my tear-stained face. I was one who would endure. Swiping the last of my tears away, I stopped crying.

Raising myself onto shaking feet, I reached tentatively toward the reflection.

How was this happening? What could it mean? I didn't have long to wonder, as the diminutive animals behind me swarmed, skittering and flapping at my back, gentle nips and pecks urging me forward, and I tumbled through the lambent archway.

Four

A FLUTTERING ENERGY gusted around me, brushing over my skin and caressing my hair. I closed my eyes, breath caught in my throat, as I stumbled out the other side of the tree's archway.

The rushing stopped. I opened my eyes and turned back to the tree to make sense of what just happened and saw the most beautiful woman in front of me. She had ice-blond hair done up in a pile of ringlets atop her pretty oval face.

A few curls fell free over her neck and bare shoulders, bouncing as she moved. She wore a sparkling silver gown with layers of ruffled silk skirts that put the bright full moon to shame with how it shimmered and glowed.

And when I stepped towards her, she moved as I moved.

Was that really me? I raised a hand to my hair, then trailed my fingers over the soft fabric of the gown. It swished around me in a soft whisper. I lifted the hem to see my holey old shoes had been swapped for slippers made from silk and silver. Oh, they felt so luxurious on my toes.

And, I was clean. Not a smudge of dirt or soot remained on me, changing the color of my skin and hair until I hardly recognized myself.

I held my hands up and did recognize the burn scars and work-worn, peeling fingertips, though. My thigh still ached softly too. It would have been nice to have seen my skin healed and smoothed as well. But I was so grateful for the rest of this transformation I hardly cared.

I was awed to see this version of who I could be, who I could have been, if I had been able to attend the ball in such finery.

But it was still only a wonderful vision, nothing more. Wasn't it? I had already missed the ball. And to confirm it, I looked up at the clock to see it tick to midnight and chime, my heart sinking low into my belly.

Then the clock's solid *tick, tick, tick* clunked roughly and sped its beat. The hands jolted, and suddenly … they were spinning fast in reverse. Midnight chimed again, and then backward time went, past eleven, ten, nine, eight …

"Is this real? If this time is true, I can still make it to

the ball," I said, as though the magic could understand me.

I stared in wonder as the clock's hands slowed and settled. "I must be back by midnight again, mustn't I? That's fine, that's more than enough. Thank you. I'll have to go through the forest, but I would have perhaps an hour there before I have to come back again."

The tree trembled, the liquid mirror of the archway rippled, and a form emerged higher than my head. It seemed at first to be part of the treasure tree itself, made of shining cogs, metal scraps, and colorful jumbled pieces, but was shaped like the muzzle of a horse. Then with a soft snort, more of a castoff bejeweled head appeared, followed by a neck trimmed in a rainbow-ribbon mane.

"Oh. You're beautiful!" I gasped, moving aside.

The strange mechanical steed stepped fully out from the glowing portal. It wore a saddle—or rather, a saddle was formed into the clockwork body of the creature itself—and knelt beside me. I took it as an invitation. The seat was wide and well-shaped, so as I sat into it with my fluffy skirts, it fit me perfectly and felt secure and stable.

My words caught on a roughness in my throat as I whispered a teary-eyed, "Thank you." Then we were moving.

The ride to the palace was a wild delight. I bellowed with uncontained thrilled laughter as we galloped under a starry sky across moonlit fields at a breakneck pace, and as

the palace came into view over a low hill, lit up like molten gold on the horizon, I felt renewed and full of awe.

On approach, I saw a long queue of carriages lined up at the main entrance and many guests entering on foot as well. My clockwork steed slowed and let me off in a shadowy grove of trees down the road. I kissed it on its large, cog-shaped cheek, then stepped out to make my way in through the gates.

Guards manned the gates, watching over the incoming crowd. Some held up scrolls that they eyed and compared against some of the women in poorer outfits, as though checking for wanted criminals. I passed through without a second look. Muffled music floated on the air, and my steps bounced in anticipation as the thought of dancing filling me with joy.

A group of women beside me apparently couldn't contain their excitement and, in a burst of shrieks and giggles, broke into a dash toward the palace. They looked like butterflies in flight, the frills of their skirts flying out behind them.

I almost joined them, but my leg still ached a little, and I knew I had to be careful and wary and not attract too much attention to myself lest my stepfamily see me.

My gown, however, wasn't cooperating with my attempts to keep people's gazes from me. Heads turned as I walked by, and I noticed more than one audible gasp as I passed up the sweeping marble staircase into the main hall.

More eyes were on me than I was comfortable with, and

A Wish of Ashes and Glass

I self-consciously tucked my scarred hands into the folds of my dress for fear that I would be recognized.

But nobody greeted me or showed signs of familiarity. Ellasyn was nobody to anybody anymore, other than a filthy, mad waif. She couldn't possibly be at the ball wearing something so magical and fine. Tonight, I may as well be somebody else. Somebody no one has met before, and will never meet again.

I followed the stream of people, and the music swelled as I stepped into the ballroom. It was a chaos of swirling skirts, bejeweled fabrics, and floating lace as dancers twirled about in unison, and the floor itself swayed, sprung timbers bouncing in time. There were simply so many women. Some men too, fathers and brothers who came as chaperones.

The gowns of those who took places through the center of the room ranged from absurdly extravagant to elegantly handsome, but there were also many others who had taken the quiet positions at the edges of the room, wearing the simple outfits of maids and merchants. It seemed all women had attended as requested, but not all had afforded a fine gown.

I gripped my fingers around the silky fabric of mine, feeling a small shame at having been blessed with this magic when so many others hadn't.

A tune came to completion, and a rousing applause filled the room as the dance ended, chased by a new melody, one that brought squeals of appreciation from those who knew it. There was something to it, a soft-edged memory from my childhood, where one marched and clapped and turned their partner, and I found my feet and heart desperately ready to dance.

I hoped my feet and heart also remembered more of the moves than my head.

It was three songs later, when my chest heaved and glimmered with sweat and my cheeks ached from smiling, that I tore myself from the music. My wounded thigh felt punished, the ache throbbing down into my knee. I knew I would suffer for this tomorrow, but for now, even that pain couldn't wipe the grin from my face.

I still had enough sense not to strain myself further, so I sought rest and refreshments. Around the edges of the huge ballroom, tables were laid out four tiers high with so many different foods I could spend a week tasting each one.

I excused myself past women muttering at how the prince hadn't yet made an appearance and helped myself to punch, a thin bar of brown cake, a cherry tart, and a scoop of fluffy cream jelly. I hadn't tasted anything like the brown cake before, but the rich sweetness of it made my eyelashes flutter, my eyes roll back, and my knees weaken.

No romance could possibly be as good as this cake. Like some kind of cake bandit, I gleefully stole three more pieces onto my plate.

I savored each sugary mouthful as I watched roaming

entertainers with glee. Sword swallowers, fire-breathers and contortionists performed tricks of magic and daring that dropped my jaw and left my heart racing.

A trumpet blared across the room, and at least one woman squealed followed by a ripple of murmuring voices. I stood on tiptoes, barely glimpsing the herald through the crowd as I licked my fingers unapologetically.

The crowd cooed and fawned as who could only be Prince Creston entered the room, trailed by a number of his sisters—Deeny, Meeny, Mornee, and Anne? I didn't know. I couldn't even count them all through the crowd.

From what I could see, though, the prince's sisters were all perfectly lovely, with skin ranging from fawn to dark sepia, like delicate dolls sparkling in their jewel encrusted gowns. There was little I could say about Prince Creston other than he wore a crown.

They followed along the edge of the ballroom, past a row of looming statues of mythic warriors that encircled the raised dais and throne where the king sat.

Prince Creston's appearance had caused the crowd to surge toward him, and I found myself standing out in the open, in the area that had been abandoned. And as the prince stepped onto the dais beside his seated father—who was invisible below the line of the crowd except for his crown—his eyes turned straight toward me.

I stood for a moment like a startled deer, cake pinched between two fingers hovering near my mouth. Then other eyes in the crowd began to follow the prince's stare. Bodies turned toward me, including two in dresses I knew too well.

Before my stepsisters' eyes could land on me, I stepped backward, ducking behind a pillar, then dashed across to an open doorway leading out of the ballroom. A long hallway stretched out empty in each direction. A sigh of relief caught in my throat and I sucked it back in as Audred's voice snapped from too close behind.

"No, we have to fix ourselves now, then go back in once we are perfect! You think all those sweaty messes out there will catch the prince's eye? Better he dances with them first so he knows what he doesn't want. Let's step out here."

Her voice grew louder, heading my way. In a panic, I tested the handle of a door across the hall and, when it turned, pushed into the dark room and closed the door gently behind me, balancing my little plate of treats carefully in my other hand. Through the timber, I could hear Terra and Dred right outside, fussing over each other's gowns, hair, and makeup.

I suppose I'm stuck in here for a while. I turned to face the murky, unlit room. At least I still had cake.

I took a small, savoring bite when a shadow moved in front of me. A voice like crushed velvet muttered, "I hope you brought some for me too."

FIVE

I BLINKED, UNABLE to make out any details in the gloom to identify the woman who spoke. A waft of smokey alcohol met my nose, and glass clinked. My stepsisters' voices still hissed through the door behind me.

I kept my voice low. "I could share a slice, if you would share this space with me for a moment."

A rustle of movement. "Do you always eat your desserts in the dark?"

"Do you always skulk in the darkness to accost unsuspecting dessert eaters?" I slammed my mouth closed too slow. Oh dear, I had spent far too long with only Dred and Terra for conversational company.

I was about to apologize but was interrupted by the barest

huff of laughter, followed by flint scraping. An oil lamp flared into life, filling the space with a soft yellow light.

The woman before me squinted her eyes at the glow she'd created and twisted the wick lower, dimming the flame. She lounged against a sideboard, eyes still on the lamp as though fascinated by the flame. She wore quilted trousers and a plain, dusty jacket, fastenings undone and hanging open over a loose white shirt. She was shockingly barefooted, and her ebony hair was braided across the sides and top of her head, falling in a tumble at the back.

The woman smirked lopsidedly as her eyes turned slowly toward me.

"There, now we can both see what we're ea—" Her gaze landed on me, and her full lips closed in a gulp. Long lashes fluttered as she blinked a few times. Then her face closed up, and she sniffed.

"You've made a lot of effort tonight. Shouldn't you be busy charming your prince out there somewhere?" A long-fingered hand waved floppily toward the door, while her other reached for a squat glass of honey liquid beside her.

"I do hope to return to enjoying the ball soon …"

My eyes were fixed on the woman as she pushed off the desk and sauntered toward me. "I'll take one of those before you leave." Her face, somehow familiar, hovered near mine as she inspected my plate of treats. "Oh, yes! These are my favorites."

A WISH OF ASHES AND GLASS

"… I'm not much interested in princes, though."

She paused, eyes the color of amber turning from the cakes to me, and her sharp eyebrows pulled together. She leaned in, and I stepped back but found myself already pressed against the door.

Her breath held a hot whiff of alcohol, and her whisper was husky. "What are you interested in, then?"

Finding myself suddenly desperately shy, it took me three attempts to get words out. "I … just … wanted a night to be free."

A moment that felt like forever later, the woman nodded once and moved away, taking a piece of cake with her. "Let us both be free, then, in our little locked-up room."

"Are you drunk?" I said, overstepping again.

The woman stabbed an accusatory finger at me. "I am *not*," she huffed, then continued, "*nearly* drunk enough to deal with this ridiculous event. All those women competing over that half-witted dolt. If they had any idea what a spoiled slob he was … Well, they'd probably all still be out there competing over him, because he's *the prince*." Her voice was mockingly childish.

The lamp flickered as she leant heavily on the hutch, casting golden light over her warm brown skin.

"I have the strangest sensation that I know you," I admitted, staring unashamedly at her. "You seem so familiar, but I can't place where I know you from. And also, I hardly know anyone."

She barked a laugh, and I winced, hoping Dred and Terra wouldn't come to inspect the noise. Pushing a decanter and a collection of books and vases carelessly away, she patted the cabinet beside her and looked up at me from under long eyelashes. "Come on, then. Come and eat cake with me, and you can tell me who I am."

A muffled grunt from behind me meant I still had time, so I hesitantly crossed the room to lean beside the woman, placing my plate down next to me. My pulse grew faster, completely silly at the mere possibility of interaction with another human that might not end in insults or punishment. I looked over her face and outfit, trying to put together the pieces.

"You're not quite dressed for riding. Some other kind of work, though. Perhaps you could be a servant here in the palace?"

Full lips twisted into a mockery of a smile. She took a greedy bite of cake and spoke around the food. "Perhaps I could be."

"But no, not with your hands." I looked over them, her fingernails straight and unchipped, skin whole and smooth. I held up mine in comparison, all broken nails, peeling fingertips, grazed knuckles. "No, these are the hands of a servant."

It was only belatedly that I saw how the lamplight made my every scar shimmer bright against my skin. The woman's whole face pinched into a frown at the sight. She reached up and closed her fingers around my wrist before I could pull away.

Her husky voice dropped an octave. "What happened to you?"

She pulled one of my hands down toward her lap, running her fingers with firm, thickened pads over my palm as she inspected the old burns and other scars.

I drew away, tucking my hands behind my back, embarrassed by them.

"An accident. When I was a child. But your hands …" A soft shiver ran over me. "They are rougher than they look—"

"Gosh, thanks," she muttered, lips on her glass.

"—with callouses on the pads and palms. Those are a sword-fighter's hands."

Her golden eyes narrowed and glimmered.

I remembered the feeling of similar, toughened-yet-gentle hands so vividly it hurt my heart.

"My father's hands felt like that. It's one of the only memories I have of him. I had been obsessed with how his sword training could change his hands so." Strange, though, for a woman … "Oh! I know who you are!"

The woman was staring at me with an intense, dark expression. "Do you?"

"Yes, I watched you—I mean, you drew my attention—I mean …" Heat rushed up my neck and ears. Why couldn't

I speak properly? "I saw you. Last week. Leading the troop of soldiers down the main road. You're a soldier or guard of some kind? I'm afraid I don't know any official terms."

The woman blinked slowly once, then smiled gently. "You got me. I'm Ara."

I beamed. "Pleasure to meet you, Ara. I'm El …" I faltered. Ellasyn was still at home, dressed in filthy rags and working through endless chores, before the time turned back to bring me here.

If there was any recognition of who I really was, if that information got back to my stepfamily, if they found out I was here at the ball, I couldn't explain to anyone how I got here if I was tasked to do so. I couldn't be Ellasyn tonight. "Just El."

"That's a very short name."

"As is yours. And besides, we've only known each other very shortly. Which I suppose is why I have the sense there is something more to you I'm missing." My gaze was trapped on her face, captivated by the dark wisps escaping and curling from her braided hairline over her temple and cheekbones.

She threw a furtive glance back at me, then threw back the last of her drink in one big swallow. Moving to refill, she lifted the bottle in offering to me, and I shook my head but felt closer to understanding this stranger.

"Is there something making you sad?" I asked softly.

A WISH OF ASHES AND GLASS

With a sigh, she shuffled her hips up onto the cabinet and sat with the bottle of alcohol clutched between her thighs. She stared at the lamp's flame again and didn't speak for a long moment, until she asked, "Your father has passed?"

"Yes, but I was very young."

Ara nodded a wobbly head. "I fear I might be faced with the same very soon. It *almost* makes me feel bad for having wished his death so many times."

"Almost?" I scolded. "I don't know how someone could wish such a thing!"

"You don't know my family." Ara leaned back to take in my aghast expression. "Don't judge me! Who are you anyway, making all these assumptions about me and my life?"

I wrung my hands together behind my back. "Have I been frightfully rude? I'm sorry, I really don't get out much."

Ara frowned but huffed a laugh at the same time. "Who *are* you?" She leaned a fraction closer, assessing me. "You, with your servant's hands yet wearing the finest gown at the ball? Where does a servant come across a dress fit for royalty?" She ran the back of a finger down a silky panel of my bodice, and my breath shuddered to a halt.

Heat bloomed through my dress at the mere thought of her touching my bare skin.

My mind fell blank. "Would you believe a tree gave it to me?"

"No."

"I'm afraid there's no other explanation I can summon for you."

Ara's fingertips lingered at the hem between bodice and skirts. How did her simple touch make my heart hammer so forcefully? Was I so starved of affection? I imagined her hand sliding across my back and wrapping around my waist to pull me closer, and it sent another wave of warmth through me.

Maybe I did have just enough energy to imagine romance after all. I hoped that in the low light, Ara couldn't see the crimson spreading over my neck and cheeks.

All mirth fell from Ara's face. "Please, tell me who you truly are."

My voice was barely a breath. "I can't."

I stood straight again and returned to the door. No sound came through other than soft music, so I cracked it open. Audred and Asterra were gone, and a clock across the hall told me that the time had passed far too quickly.

Ara moved to follow me, so I pushed the door wide. "I'm sorry. I must go. It was lovely sharing some time and cake with you. It really was."

"El, wait," Ara called.

I took off at a run, as though I could outrace my heart and the feelings I knew deep down could only lead to heartache. I had been too bold. Perhaps attending this ball at all had been foolish, giving me a taste of all the joys I would never have in my life. Foolish to wish for a night of finery that should never have been mine in the first place.

Footsteps sped after mine. I reached the ballroom and plunged into the crowd, trying to lose Ara who was still calling my name.

I was halfway across the room when a thunderous crash came from close beside me, jolting my steps. The floor shook. The music stopped, and the ballroom erupted with women's screams.

Six

SHARDS OF WHITE marble skittered across the floor near my feet. A wall of women rushed into me, pushing and tripping over each other, as a huddle of guards charged through, escorting someone in the other direction. Knocked about between the jostling bodies, I tumbled to my knees.

In front of me, a huge head, detached from its body, lay unblinking with flat, white eyes. I gasped and scrambled away from it. Other broken marble limbs and chunks lay strewn around the floor, and within the array of dismembered statue, a real man lay injured.

He moaned like a wounded steer, face down in the debris. One arm was twisted at what looked like an uncomfortable angle, jutting out from his side unnaturally, and on his shoulder, red bloomed through the gold trim of his guard's uniform.

"What's happening? I can't see! Let me through!" a gruff voice yelled from the direction of the throne. Feet rushed about all around me and the guard. I crawled a fraction closer to the injured man as panic still held the rest of the crowd in its grip.

"My arm," the man gargled out around gritted teeth.

He struggled to roll over onto his back, winced, then his eyes caught on mine, wild and pleading. "How bad? It feels bad. What can I do if I can't swing a sword? If I can't do my job …?"

My face scrunched up in sympathy, my heart reaching for him and his pain. The guard had a soft, babyish face with clean, round cheeks and pink, trembling lips. He blinked rapidly, tears clinging to long eyelashes. He seemed younger than me, and it was his fear that made my decision as much as it was his obvious pain.

"You aren't hurt nearly as bad as you think," I said loudly, hoping that if anyone watched our interaction, they'd assume the guard was overreacting rather than that his wounds had magically been healed.

I held the hand of his injured arm in mine and squeezed gently, opening my magic to help him. "There, aren't you feeling better already?"

His eyes widened, and his gaze stilled, locked onto mine.

A WISH OF ASHES AND GLASS

I knew I wasn't lying to him, not really, because he must already be feeling the effects of my healing touch.

"That's it. Just breathe. You'll get through this. Everything will be okay." Tears rushed into my own eyes, and my shoulder shuddered, stung, pain exploding as though I was run through with a sword.

I opened my mouth in a silent scream, and the guard squeezed my hand tight, with relief, confusion, instinct, I didn't know. I bit my lip as more pain shot through my body like a bolt of lightning, leaving an intense burn in its wake.

"It does. It feels better already," he muttered in awe, eyebrows twisted. "Don't cry for me, beautiful maiden."

I tried to smile back, but the agony was so intense tears splashed down heavily from my eyes.

"Tobin!" Ara appeared at my side.

The pain made my vision hazy, but I could see she had eyes only for him, her attention thankfully passing me by.

She knelt, placing her hands onto his cheeks. "What happened? Are you hurt?"

"No, it's not as bad as I thought," he murmured almost dreamily as he turned to look up into her face, brown eyes hooded affectionately.

I let go of his hand and edged away, cradling my anguished arm, trying not to move it too much for fear it would cause me to pass out. Warm liquid trickled down from my shoulder and seeped into the glowing fabric of my dress.

"Not bad? You're soaked in blood." She rolled him with ease onto his side, pulling his jacket down off his shoulder with careful intimacy.

A line of guards approached, clearing their way through the swirling, panicked crowd. I had to get out of there. I couldn't let anyone see me in my injured state. Standing was an effort so great it made me cry out and I bit down on my lip to stifle the sound.

"El?" Ara's voice was a shocked snap.

With my arms clutched close to my chest, my eyes narrowed in pain, I sped across the ballroom, agony blinding me. I gasped out apologies as I bumped and stumbled into people, the contact sending flares of torture down my injured arm. Many sneered back at my rudeness, then returned to their huddled, gossiping groups.

Cool air hit me as I burst out onto a terrace. I gulped in breaths as I raced down the stairs, each step jolting through my shoulder like a white-hot blade, and at the bottom, my clockwork horse appeared. It knelt, and I fell onto it, wrapping my uninjured arm around its neck as I whimpered into its ribbon mane.

We rode into the moonlit night. My shoulder throbbed a sickening beat in time with the horse's hooves. The ribbon mane fluttered against my face, tickling my cheek. I focused on the sensation to take my mind off the searing ache in my arm.

In the distance, I heard a clock bell strike. An unnatural breeze lifted around me, and panic rose in my throat, stifling my already labored breaths.

The clock had struck five times when the tree came into view.

Six and seven as my clockwork horse skidded to a stop before it and knelt.

Eight, nine as I fought the excruciating pain that threatened to pull me under as I clambered from its back.

Ten, eleven, I dashed through the shimmering doorway, the cool mirrored barrier washing over me.

On the stroke of twelve, I stumbled out the other side. I fell into the long grass between the graves, screaming as my arm hit the ground. I rolled to my good side, heart pounding, nerves singing in agony, and everything was back to normal.

Gone was the beautiful silver gown and the elegant slippers the tree had gifted me. In their place were my dingy gray work dress and old worn shoes. My hair was back in a dirty bun with no sign of golden curls anywhere. The horse had followed me through the doorway and vanished too.

I pushed myself up with my good arm and sat on the graves, catching my breath, wondering if I had dreamed it all. Still, I had kept one souvenir from my glorious night.

"Ow …" I whimpered, more tears springing to my eyes. I explored gingerly around my shoulder with my other hand, my fingers feeling the blood already coming through my servant's dress. I felt faint, my head spinning as I pressed through the fabric against ragged, stinging flesh.

The tear felt muscle-deep, and I worried I had taken on too much. That this time the injury was too severe. Would I lose much motion in that arm? I had no duty to swing a sword, but so many of my chores required functioning limbs. I needed to get inside to my quarters to tend to my new wound.

I wobbled slowly to my feet, looking up at the treasure tree and its branches spread above me. Its trunk had closed, and it appeared no different to usual, sea glass and porcelain shards shimmering in the moonlight between jingling metal.

Despite everything—the exhaustingly long day, the pain, the dramatic ending to the night—I somehow felt renewed. As though a spark of warmth and joy had reignited somewhere inside me.

"Is that part of your magic as well?" I whispered to the tree.

I wasn't a stranger to magic, but it was ever as incomprehensible as it was wondrous. All the women of my family had some sort of gift, since my great-grandmother. She and my grandmother both had magical powers, then my mother never seemed to come into a gift, and they thought it was over until I displayed mine.

As I made my way up the path back toward home, humming a tune I had danced to that night, I wondered whether my mother's gift was being displayed now, through the treasure tree. That tonight had been an enchanted present from her. I felt warm inside at the idea that she was still watching over me.

But a chill had settled inside as well. How was I supposed to go on enduring my cruel life if that was the last show of kindness I would ever know?

For a few short moments at the ball, when Ara had gazed with such a sweet intensity into my eyes, I had almost hoped for something more …

Yet she had all that tenderness and more for the injured guard, Tobin. And who was I to her? Nobody she could ever know.

I would only be punishing myself by wishing I would ever see her again.

But punish myself, I did.

SEVEN

THERE WOULD BE another ball.

The announcement came within days of the first, with the event to be held a week from then.

Dred and Terra had spent the time since the first ball relating to me in repetition the drama of the night and the incredible tragedy that the statue falling over had put a stop to proceedings right as Audred was about to dance with Prince Creston.

Audred swooned at the news of another ball. "Honestly, I can't tell if I am cursed to always have some incident keep the prince from my reach, or if the fates favor me with these second chances. And so little time to prepare another gown!"

Of course she thought the world, all fates and curses, revolved around her. I may even have said as much were we not all standing in line before Lord Trolaine, myself a step back from his daughters.

He had intercepted the invitation this time and called us into his study to pass on the news. It was hot and stuffy, as he insisted a fire to always be burning in the large open fireplace. We used more wood in there than we did in the hearth.

Trolaine eyed me almost greedily. "Do you wish for another chance to attend the ball?"

I did. I desperately did. But how could I say so without giving my stepfather more ammunition to use against me?

The moment I heard the news of a second ball, my first thought was of Ara, whether I might see her again. But I wasn't fool enough to think Trolaine ever intended to let me go the first time, nor would he allow me to meet the requirements this time if we made the same deal.

Last time, if there had been some punishment for not attending, our agreement could probably have been used as proof it had been my fault for not going. But as nobody came knocking to see why I wasn't there—although indeed I had been—Trolaine would have even less incentive to let me go.

I couldn't see a reason to play that game with Trolaine again and take on all the extra work for nothing. Instead, I should resign myself to the fact that such luxuries are not something I should wish for.

"No, my lord. Such an event isn't the place for me."

A WISH OF ASHES AND GLASS

He smiled toothily in a way that lifted his bushy red moustache. He had the look of a predator when he said, "Quite. But if one of my daughters is marrying into royalty soon, we need the manor looking its best. And as you were able to get a decent amount of work done last week, there's no reason you can't always get that much done."

My spirits dropped like a stone into a dry well. I had been too naive. The game had already been played and I had lost. Daring to show my interest in the first ball had locked me into a greater workload for good. I could not backtrack and say if I was doing the work anyway, then I'd wish to attend the ball. He would be sure to pile on more chores again. I couldn't say anything that would work out in my favor.

I simply grit my teeth, curtseyed, and was dismissed with relief.

As far as fates and curses went, I wondered whether I should make any attempt to attend another ball lest I were tempting more pain into my life. It was such a risk. The chance of being identified and my presence there reported to Trolaine, or being spotted by him or my stepsisters directly, could lead to a terrible punishment.

And what if there was another accident? After the carriage hitting the child, then the statue falling, it seemed every journey outside my home was fraught with events that tested my promise to always help those whose suffering I could take on.

My shoulder was healing well, remarkably well. It had transferred from the guard to me exactly, as we weren't much different in size, and I had feared I'd taken on too much, that I might lose some movement or feeling forever from the torn muscles and nerves. But the wound closed well and showed no signs of redness or rot, and even the pain subsided far faster than I would have thought. And I had been proud that I'd held to my vow and healed the man.

But the next time I was witness to suffering, how far could I go to heal it? How much more could my body and spirit take? Perhaps it was better to keep myself away from situations where my vow would be tested.

Then again, the chances of another accident had to be very low. Beyond a few blistered heels, a ball at the palace had to be one of the safest places to be with the king's guard around. And even so, I would risk it to see Ara again. Not only has my shoulder ached from the injury, but my heart has ached at the mere thought of her.

My mind turned these tumbling circles as I ran the laundry through the wringer, cranking the handle with my good arm.

What was it about Ara that had bewitched me so? The simple fact she spoke with me not as a lord would to a servant? That she saw my scars and hadn't turned away?

I held a warm tightness in my chest ever since the first ball, and every night as I lay in my small cot in the cellar,

A WISH OF ASHES AND GLASS

I would close my eyes and feel Ara's fingertips at my waist, see the gentle smirk on her pouting lips, hear the shielded vulnerability in her warm voice.

I hadn't been prepared, that first ball, to really engage with anyone. Hadn't considered how to protect my identity and had made mistakes, panicked, and made it worse by fleeing. But that even more made me want to see Ara again, to apologize and explain—as much as I was able to while keeping my secrets.

I scolded myself away from any thoughts that we could have more than a few pleasant hours in each other's company anyway, if she even was there, if she even wanted *my* company again. There was such an insurmountable mountain of ifs.

But as the week progressed, I found it was my thoughts of Ara, the building desire to see her again, even if for a moment, that was all that distracted me from my life and got me through the backbreaking work each day.

I didn't dare assume I would be blessed with gifts from my treasure tree again, so I found time to finish my dress, working on it late into the evenings by the dim light of the kitchen hearth after all others were asleep.

The pastel lilac fabric from the old curtains came up nicely with a few copper buttons from my tree, and although the design was simple, it was something I could hold my head up proudly in knowing I created something for myself.

The night of the second ball arrived, and I knew my plan better than the scars on my hands. I would wait until Trolaine, Terra, and Dred had left, then prepare myself and make my way on foot to the ball. I would arrive late, no doubt, and tomorrow morning, I would face Trolaine's punishment for tonight's list of chores that would go undone.

But somehow, that seemed less terrible than not making the attempt to see Ara again.

I helped my stepsisters into the new gowns their father had bought for them. He must have paid a fortune, as, unsurprisingly, the value of dresses in Estoria had shot up dramatically. I caught Audred staring at her flower-embroidered bodice with a look less like excitement and more like how one would eye the hangman's noose.

She muttered to herself and snapped at me, making me redo her hair three times, then redoing Asterra's hair herself.

She stuttered almost hysterically, "If not me, if not … One of us must, at least … at least, one of us must. We cannot fail at this."

I pressed my lips together and helped as I could in silence, as my concern for her grew.

Then Trolaine called for me from downstairs, and I excused myself. I found him in the kitchen, standing before the worktable, his hand upon a stack of roughly cut, fabric squares. They were lilac in color.

A WISH OF ASHES AND GLASS

My fingers went cold and my ribcage seemed to contract, threatening to squeeze my heart to a stop. *Is that my gown?*

"I have a gift for you here." Trolaine lifted a wad of the fabric sheets that had just hours before been my finished dress.

I couldn't speak. My jaw shook. The backs of my eyes burned but I refused to shed a tear in front of this horrid man.

"Come now? Where is the gratitude? You should appreciate these new washcloths I've provided you."

My dress. My fingertips still felt raw from pushing the needle and tugging the thread all those hours.

Trolaine slapped the wad he held back onto the pile, then stepped close, staring down his nose at me. "I expect you to use them to scrub the filthiest parts of the house. Then perhaps you will also see the gift I am giving you of a lesson. That you should never have dared spend your time on a task that I have not assigned for you, and that disobedience will not be tolerated. Show me you understand these gifts. Say 'thank you, my lord'."

I opened my mouth and choked on clogged up tears.

He snatched a poker from beside the hearth and smacked it against the table leg. "SAY IT!"

"Thankyoumylord," I gasped out.

He dropped the poker onto the ground and marched out. As he left through the door, I heard him mutter, "As though you could ever have been competition for my daughters in

that dress of scraps."

I stood there, numbness filling every part of me, as the bustling noises of Trolaine and his daughters leaving by carriage echoed through the house.

Then I rushed to the table and clutched at the fabric scraps, laying them out. Could I sew them back together? Tears finally spilled over and splattered down, creating dark spots on the lilac. Even if I could sew faster than any living creature, I would look like I was wearing a quilt of squares.

For a moment, I considered stealing one of my stepsister's dresses, but wearing their clothes would only increase my chances of being recognized and then having to endure the punishment afterward. My mother's gowns had been sold years before, as though my stepfamily hadn't wanted any trace of her left behind.

Could I simply go to the ball as I was? And stand in the corner, ashamed, as the other women who hadn't been able to afford grand ballgowns did last time? Even then, their servant uniforms were far neater than the scraps I wore. I would be humiliated.

I slumped, sadness rippling through me. I would not go to the ball. I would not see Ara again.

I picked up the fabric squares and tossed them into my cleaning bucket, staring with dull eyes as they drifted down beneath the water. Then I began working through my list of chores, and every time I wrung out the cloth, my chest ached at the reminder of my foolish wishes.

Still, if I couldn't go to the ball, there was no reason for me to take punishment tomorrow for not getting Trolaine's tasks completed.

It was dark by the time I was done, and my every muscle felt stiff and tired, but my mind swirled in outrage and grief and wouldn't let me rest, so I made my way down to my parents' graves and the treasure tree in search of a little solace.

I stood before the spangled limbs, breath caught in my throat as a wave of hope came over me. But as I stared up at the clock, nothing happened. I shouldn't have dared to hope. I sniffed away my tears and lay down beside Mamma's grave, spent and empty.

I must have fallen asleep, because I came to with a start as the clock above chimed. Midnight, hours after I'd laid myself there. I squinted my sleep-sore eyes away from the brightness. A brightness caused by a building glow. Then the tree shifted and twisted as magic formed a miracle for me again, splitting the tree down the center as before.

Breathless, I stood and needed no prompting this time to step through the sparkling, liquid doorway.

I closed my eyes as the magic flowed around me, my heart racing as my overworked muscles were revived and the tiredness ebbed away, leaving me refreshed. When the energy stopped and I opened my eyes again, I found myself looking at a reflection that was so bright and blinding I had to blink to bring the image before me into focus. I had been gilded, spun into gold.

The gown flowed around me like an egg-yolk sun, in satin so glossy it could be molten metal. Intricate lace swirled up my chest and over my shoulders, hiding my healing wound. The skirt had pleats and folds that whispered as I spun before my reflection. My hair was pinned up in a crown of curls with golden pins that glittered like sunlight through spring leaves.

The clock chimed twelve before rewinding to eight, and my clockwork steed emerged and knelt before me.

"Thank you," I whispered, as I reached out and ran my fingers through its ribbon mane, awed and so grateful that such magic had been bestowed upon me a second time.

I would try to be worthy of its gift, although I wasn't sure how exactly to do that. When there had been so many hardships in my life, why bless me now? Why bless me with gifts that only allowed me a few hours of peace and joy at a royal ball? Did the magic want me to try to win the competition that was the reason for the events? Win the hand of the prince? Doing so would remove me from the awful situation here with Trolaine but still seemed to me it would be yet another form of servitude.

I reached the ball on the gallop of bric-a-brac legs, kissed my thanks on a metal cheek, and walked up through the front gates.

A WISH OF ASHES AND GLASS

The entryway into the ballroom had changed since the first night and this time led all women through an entrance that paraded us in front of the royal family seated on their thrones.

I became enthralled by a fire-breather who performed nearby, drawing candles from his cart that he lit up with flame from his mouth. These candles he would then make vanish within his palms, only to make them reappear, still lit, from the folds of women's gowns, leaving them squealing with fear and mirth.

The line shuffled closer to the king and prince, who were backed by a line of countless princesses and a ring of guards. I shot a look at the remaining marble statues, warning them not to move and hoping there wouldn't be a repeat of the events from the last ball. So distracted, I stumbled in my gold slippers when Trolaine's voice boomed from just a few places ahead in the parade.

I ducked behind the woman in front of me, trying to hide my face as I peeked around her. The chances of Trolaine and my stepsisters seeing me seemed low, as they only had eyes for King Othon and Prince Creston. Trolaine stepped up to the dais, schmoozing an introduction of Audred, then Asterra in a slow, fawning way that had the rest of the waiting line growing tense.

This close, I had my first good look at the royal father and son.

King Othon looked unwell and far older than his years. His dark skin was highlighted in a sickly gray, and mauve bruises hung under each bloodshot eye. He made no reply to Trolaine beyond waving him away with one crooked hand while keeping his gaze fixed on the parade of guests. Prince Creston was younger than I had imagined, more a child than a man, with a dull, pouting demeanor and a teenager's rose-spotted cheeks.

Audred and Asterra stood in prim terror behind their father as he boasted their virtues. Creston had his eyes on them, still dull and pouting, and my stepsisters contorted their faces into their best forced smiles. Othon waved more furiously as Trolaine blocked his view, and a man in flowing purple robes with neat white hair and a nose like a hook emerged from the shadows behind the thrones. He approached Trolaine, attempting—and failing—to politely push him on his way.

Audred and Asterra turned redder in the cheeks than their father's moustache, but their brittle, unhappy smiles didn't crack.

The couple of people in front of me started moving again, determined to pass the king and prince despite Trolaine refusing to move on, and those behind me started to push forward too, directing me right beneath the noses of my stepfamily.

I tried to excuse myself nonchalantly, to let others before me in line as I ducked backward, to make some excuse for not moving forward.

Then strong, hard fingers closed around my wrist, sending a shudder of surprise through my chest. It was the hand of a guard, their black and gold uniform crisp and intimidating. I was dragged out of line, confused, but grateful at least that I was moved away from my stepfamily.

Stumbling, I looked up into Ara's eyes and found no kindness there.

"Why did you run?"

"Sorry?"

There was no patience in her eyes either. "Why did you flee the last ball?"

Ara dragged me further away from the parade, away from the dais, and down an empty hallway. At least I was completely out of sight of my stepfamily. But I didn't like how she was looking at me. It made my lips tremble so hard it was difficult to speak.

Ara said more softly, "Were you *hurt*?"

"No. I … ran because some of the guard's blood got on me, and I panicked." With courage, I added, "Why does it matter that I left after the accident?"

Ara sighed. "Because I don't believe it was just an accident."

EIGHT

ARA'S BRONZE FINGERS still circled around my wrist, her grip gentle but unrelenting.

"Not an accident? What else, then?" My voice came out breathy.

Casting her gaze back down the hallway, her eyes flicking around as though hunting for enemies, she turned the other way, striding along with me in tow. "An attack. An attempt upon the king's life."

I clip-clopped in my gold slippers to keep up and pictured the ring of majestic marble figures in my mind. "The statue fell near the dais but not close enough to ever threaten the king himself."

"A clumsy attempt, a failed attempt, but an attempt no

less. I refuse to believe it was an accident, but I have no proof. Beyond the simple logic that marble statues that have stood firm for generations rarely topple like a twelve-year-old who stole too much ale from the larders and drank it all on the roof of the gazebo."

"That's an oddly specific comparison. But why, beyond the improbability of toppling statuary, would it not be an accident? Why would someone try to hurt the king?"

Ara gave an exasperated shake of her head as though it was an obvious answer, too obvious to put into words.

Her hair was held back in the same rows of braids across the top and sides of her head as last time but now pulled into a tight bun at the back. The high-collared uniform of thick, quilted black velvet, studded with gold clasps and trim, hugged tight across her narrow waist and up tense shoulders.

Her fingers slid from my wrist and down to hold my hand, sending a small thrill to my chest. She turned us around a corner, pushed through a door, and led me down into a storage cellar.

"Where are we going?" I asked despite it not mattering in the slightest. With her hand in mine, I felt I would follow Ara anywhere. My body thrummed with energy, fuelled by her touch.

We were only a few steps in when there was a sound up ahead. Ara muttered a curse. She scooped me round the waist in a way that made me gasp and carried me bodily down a narrow aisle of wooden barrels.

As footsteps approached, Ara looked me up and down, sighed almost wistfully, and hissed, "You are brighter than a summer's day."

"Apologies. I hadn't planned for hiding in a cellar when I was dressed," I whispered back.

Ara bundled the bulk of my skirts into her arms then pressed them between her body and mine, as though she could hide me entirely beneath her own dark apparel.

She turned her head, peering through a gap between the barrels. Leaned in as she was, the long line of her neck up to her ear was close to my lips, and my breath shivered. My whole body thrummed at the thought of closing that small gap and pressing my mouth to her smooth skin.

Lit lanterns lined the wall opposite us, creating a warm glow, and another moving light reflected off the ceiling near the other end of the long room. Soft footsteps and muffled muttering interspersed the sounds of rummaging through stores.

I kept my voice as silent as a breath. "What are we doing here? You're a guard. Why are you hiding?"

She shifted, moving to bring her face close beside mine. Her lips brushed my ear, making it tingle, as she whispered, "I *may* have been ordered not to explore my suspicions. Which only makes me more suspicious that I'm not the only one with suspicions and that those others have listed me as someone to be suspicious of."

"That's a lot of suspicions."

"And so, I don't want to be caught sneaking around, since I already could be seen as having motivation."

"What motivation would you—"

"Hush." Ara pressed two fingers against my lips. The wavering light had moved closer. It came our way, and Ara held my gaze, and I wondered what must she think of how I trembled under her touch. Surely she could feel the effect she was having on me.

As the light passed by the end of the aisle we hid in, Ara half-turned her face away to look.

Over her shoulder, I saw the man in purple robes that had been near the king earlier. He carried a swinging lantern in one hand and a wrapped bundle under his arm. He didn't glance our way as he trotted by on skittish feet.

Ara hmphed. "It's only Hareth."

"Who?"

"The king's advisor."

"And does he warrant your suspicions?"

Ara turned back to me. "Hareth? No, I can't think of any motive he could possibly have. He's always been completely loyal to Othon."

"You seem awfully familiar with everyone."

A Wish of Ashes and Glass

Ara lazily lifted and dropped a shoulder. "Comes with my role."

As the door closed behind the man, Ara's body softened against mine, but she didn't step back. Her dark eyebrows crept together, and she pierced me with her golden gaze.

"I thought I saw you bleeding when you fled the last ball." Ara lifted a hand and brushed it over the lace on my shoulder. I made every effort not to flinch as she passed over the still-healing wound beneath.

She frowned deeply. "And there was so much blood spilled. But how to account for it? Tobin, who had howled like the wind out of a ghost's arse, hasn't got a scratch on him. He can't seem to explain how. I'm at a loss."

I aimed to distract her from that mystery. "Is he ... Are you close with Tobin?"

Ara huffed a laugh. "I do tend to keep him closer under my eye than the other guards, mostly due to how incredibly accident prone the boy is and that I couldn't face his mother if I let him skewer himself on his own whetstone."

I quirked my eyebrows. "Not his sword?"

"You underestimate Tobin's capacity for improbable self-harm."

She shook her head, then, as though blinking out of a reverie, stepped back, letting my gown fall free. It swept to the floor between us in a swish of satin.

Ara swallowed and stared at the shining gold. "My point, though, is that I'm faced with so many mysteries, and I've always been better with a sword than politics and intrigue. At the first ball, you showed you had the wit of an investigator, and I hoped that you might help me."

"I'd be happy to. Although it would have been nice to be asked before being dragged halfway across the castle."

Ara met my eyes for a moment before dropping them back to my skirts. "Forgive me. I am … distracted."

"I'm teasing. Your poorest manners are bliss compared to my normal treatment."

This only made Ara frown more.

My cheeks flushed hot at my poorly chosen words. I did not want her pity, so I turned to take in our surroundings. "To the task, then. Why are we here? And why would anyone want to hurt the king?"

Ara tilted her head, leading me out of the aisle. "I heard this is where they've stored the broken statue. They cleaned it all away so fast. I hoped to have a look, to see if it held some clues."

She strode down the storeroom, plucking at crates and peering over shelves. "As for the king, there are many who would see him gone and have little patience to wait for nature to take its course. There's a reason Estoria is the richest of all kingdoms, and the reason is military aggression. Othon has been pushing the limits right up to the brink of open warfare for years now. I hate how he uses my soldiers so."

"Your soldiers?"

Ara shrugged. "Managing the military falls under my purview, the day to day running of it, not so much its exploitation. Just part of my work for which I receive no credit."

I had no idea Ara was so highly ranked, but I could empathise with receiving no credit for one's efforts. "What would you do with the military if you could decide the use of it?"

Ara paused with her hands on the lid of a wooden box. "You would be interested?"

"I'd love to hear you speak of it."

It was hard to tell in the low light, but it seemed that Ara's sepia cheeks had turned rosy. Her eyes sparkled.

"So many things. With a force like that, that number of bodies working toward one cause, there is so much we could build, or create, rather than destroy." Her voice grew strong and animated, humming with passion. "There are so many roles within the city that need that sort of support, helping our people rather than lining our coffers."

Then Ara's voice dropped, the enthusiasm waning. "There is so much I would do. But I never could, because I will never be king." Then rushed at the end she added, "Obviously."

"That sounds amazing, though. Perhaps you could speak with the king and share your ideas?"

Ara half smiled, huffing her breathy laugh. She turned away from me, continuing her search of the shelves. "Oh no. Nobody likes to hear my ideas. Least of all the king himself. It's nice, though, that you did. Thank you, for listening. But I do wish you would tell me more about yourself."

"Oh, I think you would find me frightfully dull if I let fall my veil of mystery."

"I can't imagine I would ever find you dull." She turned back to me, locking eyes with mine for a second that felt like the length and warmth of summer.

I swallowed with a dry mouth. Her attention made me feel like everything and nothing all in one moment. It made every part of my body come alive, made everything about life seem full of hope and promise, but in the same breath made my heart ache at the knowledge that these moments would all come to nothing, in the end.

How could I let myself believe we could have more than these brief hours of subtle touches and kind words, ticking down until a looming midnight? It couldn't be possible while my secrets divided us. I had to just take what joy I could in the present.

"What's under there?" I pointed to a hessian sheet in the back corner of the storeroom to distract her.

Ara lifted it, and beneath lay a jumble of pale body parts.

"There you are," Ara murmured, as though she'd won a

game of hide-and-seek against the pieces of marble.

We crouched before the broken statue, looking over the chipped and shattered sections. Each limb was as wide around as my torso, and I couldn't shift them myself, but Ara picked them up one by one and spread them out across the floor for inspection.

I ran my fingers over the hard marble, the clean breaks where it had split apart when it toppled. "You said before about the king, about nature taking its course. What did you mean?"

"How the king is unwell," Ara said matter-of-factly. When I returned a look of surprise, she continued. "Has been for some time. Seems strange to attempt to harm a man who hasn't much longer to live. It had been kept secret for a while, but his recent trip out of the palace seems to have spread the news across the kingdom."

I had seen King Othon that night, and he seemed worn and tired, but I hadn't thought he'd be so close to death. "I didn't know."

"You do seem remarkably immune to royal gossip for someone dressed so finely. Well, his trip was in the hopes of acquiring a cure, but it was not as promised, so those who wish him dead really ought to just show a little patience."

The ground where the statue pieces had been piled before caught my attention. It seemed unusually dusty to an eye trained to banish any filth on sight. I swept my hands over the stone floor.

A soft powder met my touch, with some larger chalky pieces that crumbled as I pressed them between my fingers. That wasn't marble. "As odd as it seems that someone would want a dying man dead faster—long live the king—I think you might be onto something."

"What have you found?"

The color of powder on my fingers was a brighter white than the gray-streaked marble of the statue, and I quickly spotted a matching patch on one of the statue's ankles. "This section of marble has been replaced with some softer stone. Look." I pressed my fingertips into an already cracked section, and it crumbled easily.

Ara crouched beside me and ran her hands over it. "It looks like talc. This wasn't an accident." Her voice was low and firm as a frown darkened her features. "It's almost seamless—I wouldn't have even noticed. How on earth did you spot that?"

"It was the sweepings. A place only a servant used to cleaning might look, I suppose."

Ara shook her head at me, mouth gaping. "El, you *must* tell me who you are. But first, we must tell the king of the threat." She reached a hand for mine, and I met it halfway, clutching tight. We broke into a run.

Ara led me at a bracing pace back the way we had come. We pushed out into the ballroom, barging through toward the dais. We were tangled and whipped by passing dresses, silky fabric and hooped skirts hindering our passage. I was losing grip already on the battering ram Ara had become, lost in the frilly wake behind her, when I was grasped by my free hand and wrenched out of Ara's grip.

I was yanked to a halt, my injured shoulder straining in a way that brought tears to my eyes and a silent yelp to my throat. Ara had disappeared out of sight, her mission far greater than who she had left behind. I turned to identify my captor—Trolaine? Dred? Terra?

It was Prince Creston.

"Where were you going, in such haste?" He eyed me warily.

"Your Highness." I dipped a swift curtsey, ducking my head to hide my face lest Dred and Terra had the prince in their sights.

"Get up. Tell me what you were doing with *her*?"

I was saved from answering him when the crack of an explosion ripped across the room.

Nine

ORANGE LIGHT FLASHED, and a burst of heat washed over the room. Another burst of flame whoofed, this time smaller, eclipsed by screams and stampeding feet.

Prince Creston let me go, and people pushed all around, the prince taken away in the throng. I didn't know which way to move, as the crowd flowed in all directions, pulling me one way and then another while people rushed for any escape or cover.

A crackling series of explosions continued, like fireworks going off inside, deafening, and the panicked crowd jammed the doorways, blocking the exits as too many people tried to escape at once.

What is happening? Could this be another planned attack?

A view cleared to the affected area, close to the dais, but again not close enough to threaten the king, who still sat hunched on his throne and cast glaring eyes about the space.

Guards, led by Ara, charged into that space, stomping out flames and smoldering patches that marred the dancefloor. A cart decorated with painted flames lay on its side, the top blown out and smoking. I breathed a sigh of relief that nobody lay prone in that area, nobody seemed hurt and in pain.

"The fire-breather! Find the fire-breather!" the king yelled.

My eyes sought Ara, staring at her for a long moment, wishing I could help her more. Then I backed away, hoping to find an unblocked exit so I could slip out, as midnight surely approached. But the guards moved rapidly, taking a doorway each themselves and checking all who tried to leave.

I moved past a table, where the piles of food had fallen in an avalanche to the floor, and tripped on something firm. Clutching at the table to steady myself, I looked back to see a leg, then a body, scorched black with soot that also trailed back across the ground he must have been blasted over.

The fire-breather. I'd watched him earlier in the night, his clever magic with his hands and breath. Now, he curled, whimpering, holding blistered fingers before a face twisted with pain, fear and confusion.

An icicle grew sharp and frosty in my chest. I knew. I knew exactly the pain this man was in. The scars that covered my hands and wrists would never let me forget, the first time my gift had presented itself, and my skin tingled with the memory of it.

Mamma, on all fours near the bed, crying as cinders and ash settled around her. Tripped over, her hands plunged into the burning contents of the warming pan she had carried, spilled around her. Me, four, maybe five, knowing I only wanted to make it better. And I had. And it cost me.

When Mamma realized what I'd done, she knew how dangerous my gift could be. She made me promise to keep it secret. The memory itself was blurry, but the recollection of the pain it caused was not.

The searing, bone-deep sting of burns. I felt sick inside to even imagine it. To contemplate what this man was going through. To know that I could fix it and take it all away.

"Where is he? Don't let him get away!" It was Ara this time, yelling orders across the space.

I should call Ara over, tell someone he's here. Whatever plot was unfolding, this fire-breather was clearly the prime suspect now. But the memory of my burns paralyzed me, and there was something more. The anguish on his face gave me pause.

He noticed me then, staring at him in frozen horror.

"What happened? How …?" His voice came out rough, choked with agony. "My fire … it couldn't, it shouldn't … Was anyone else hurt?"

I took in the crumpled man before me. He was terrified, distressed, delirious with pain. No, I couldn't believe he'd done this on purpose. But could I trust others to come to the same conclusion? Ara maybe, but the king had jumped straight to accusing the fire-breather.

I hid the fire-breather with my skirts and pleaded, "Can you run? Please, you should run lest they blame this and more on you."

His attention had returned to his scorched hands, shaking before his face. He gagged stuttering breaths and squeezed his eyes shut, lost in pain.

My lips twisted. I didn't want to do it. I feared it. That memory kept pushing back into my mind and making my stomach roil.

You can do this. If you don't do this, he will lose the magic of his hands at the least, and at the most, his life, if he is thought to have attacked the king.

I had to give him the chance to escape. I was already crying, tears burning my eyes, before I bent down, reached out a hand, and touched the man's cheek. "It's going to be all right."

Then there was screaming. Gasping, hard-edged screams. They came from my throat, and I couldn't control them. Couldn't stop them. My vision blurred out, and I was stumbling, reeling back. It felt as though the skin was being melted from my finger bones, and that pain blasted up my arms. Pulsing, sickening waves flowed into my heart and filled my chest and skull.

I was caught from behind and turned around by hard hands.

"El? You're hurt! Were you so close to the explosion?" Ara took me in, my hands held shaking before me, fingers curled, the tears pouring from wild eyes. She scooped me into her arms.

Over her shoulder, a nearby door had been left unguarded—hers, no doubt, as she'd stepped away to reach me—and I watched as the fire-breather slipped through. He glanced back at me for just a moment, his eyes wide, before disappearing.

Ara carried me toward a different door, barking at the guard and crowd surrounding it, "Clear the way!"

Everything swirled as agony ripped away my senses. We were moving. I lolled against Ara's soft chest, held crushed within her arms. A door was kicked open. I was laid on a leather lounge.

"I'll be right back. I'm going to get a doctor."

There was a gentle touch to my forehead, then she was gone.

I blinked the tears from my eyes, heard the *tick, tick, tick* of a clock somewhere above me. It was almost midnight. I had to get out of there.

With a howl of anguish, I rolled up into a sitting position, forced myself onto my feet, and rushed blindly for an exit. I didn't know where I was on the palace grounds or how to find my way. I cried out with relief when my magical horse appeared the moment I was outside.

I leaned and lay on the horse's back, unable to hold on with my hands, and it sped me home.

I DON'T KNOW how I made it from the tree back into the house and into bed. The journey was a blur, and I didn't recall much of the night after taking on the fire-breather's wounds. Only pain. So much pain. As though pain would be all I'd ever know. All I would ever be cursed with.

But I awoke the next morning, and my mind was clear. My body again felt refreshed, as though I'd slept a hundred years. My hands stung bitterly, the deep heat still burning beneath the scorched flesh. But there were already signs they were healing, sections where the blisters peeled away to show fresh pink skin beneath. Still, the remaining wounds made all my morning chores excruciating.

I feared punishment at being slow at setting breakfast again, but the rest of the family slept late and wandered in yawning without a question to the time.

"What a night!" Audred exclaimed as she reached for a slice of fresh bread. "Oh, Cinders, did you miss out on the drama!"

I quirked my eyebrows. "Did I? What happened?"

"Someone tried to blow up the king!" Asterra interrupted

Audred to a replied flash of anger.

"Surely not," I replied.

Trolaine joined us then, and the sisters drew themselves in, postures fixed, faces set into their placating smiles, and voices silenced.

"Don't show yourself to be so excited by tragedy, or one might think you wish the king to pass," he scolded them.

Asterra offered very timidly, "It would, though, make Prince Creston the king, which would make the one he chooses to marry his queen."

Trolaine smacked his lips, and his moustache quivered. "That it would. And we made our good impression on him last night."

I withheld a scoff.

"I feel he didn't much show interest in me." Audred sounded exhausted. "But it almost seemed that he didn't show much interest in anyone. Do you think there will be another ball?"

Asterra muttered, "There was that one woman he chased after right before the explosion. The one in the beautiful golden dress."

I stiffened, holding my breath, but nobody turned to accuse me.

"I heard others saying they saw the same mystery woman fleeing after the statue fell as well," Asterra added.

Audred perked up a little, drawn into the intrigue. "Not one of the princesses? There are so many I can hardly keep track. But I heard someone saying the king's daughters may be suspects. Which seems ridiculous to me, since the king's death would only make Creston king."

"And surely Creston would not harm his father, with him being so ill anyway," Asterra nodded back.

"*Surely* all of this is gossip and hearsay that is beneath us!" Trolaine wiped his mouth on a napkin and thumped it back to the table. "It's clear that the attack last night was by the fire-breather. Whether he had accomplices or not matters little to us."

The sisters stilled as Trolaine snapped his fingers at me for a refill of his tea.

But Asterra's eyes widened until she blurted out, "But what if the attacks weren't meant to hurt the king, but instead Prince Creston!"

Trolaine frowned, and I was worried for Asterra as I took the teapot in my stinging fingers and poured. My hand shook, and the spout clinked and chattered against the cup.

But Trolaine didn't declare punishment, instead saying softly, "They were always much closer to the prince than to the king." Then, with his eyes turned my way and voice raised, "What is this disgusting mess of your hands you are presenting me with!"

A WISH OF ASHES AND GLASS

I set the teapot down carefully and backed away. "I spilled hot water last night and was burned. I'm sorry, I haven't been able to wrap them myself." I had tried, but when each hand ached as fiercely as the other, my attempts to bandage them ended in pain and frustration.

Trolaine stared at me long and hard, then as though too disgusted to eat another bite, he threw his cutlery to the table and left.

Audred pushed her chair back just as fast but came over to stand in front of me. "Must you be such a terrible klutz, Cinders? Show me."

I held my hands out, and she cringed, crinkling her nose, then she marched off to the kitchen.

"Sit," she commanded on return, carrying a roll of muslin strips and a jar of ointment. I took a seat, and she crouched in front of me, scooping the sticky, pungent gel with her fingers and dabbing it onto my burns none too gently. I winced and bit my tongue, not wanting to interrupt her show of kindness despite her roughness.

Audred tsked. "You really must try harder. This is no way to be a good daughter, or a good woman. You're lucky Father didn't punish you. And you'd deserve it too. No, don't look at me like that, Terra! She would. She's not trying nearly hard enough to be someone who could be married, and if she isn't married, how is she ever to be more than a servant?"

"Do you *really* think I could ever be more than a servant?"

Audred pursed her lips, silent for a moment, then said low, "Sometimes I hope it for you. But not if you keep insisting on covering yourself in scars until your value is completely lost."

"I meant," I said softly, "do you truly think your father would ever allow it?"

Audred's lip twitched, but she said nothing as she wrapped the thin fabric around my wrist and over my palm. We all sat in silence, our words hanging heavily between us, as she bandaged the other hand and pinned it securely.

"Come, Terra. There is sure to be another ball, and we must start planning immediately."

Asterra gave me a small, pouting expression as they moved to leave but turned her eyes quickly after her sister. Audred paused in the doorframe and called back, "Father only wants what's best for us, and we must in return do our best to meet that challenge and achieve his dreams for us."

An unexpected tear fell from my eye as I stared at the neat bandaging she'd done for me. "What about your dreams?"

But they were gone.

THE REST OF the week passed with no announcement of another ball. Still, Dred and Terra were in remarkably good

spirits, although they bickered more as well, snapping at each other in hushed whispers as they scurried around the house.

My hands healed well, and once, when no one else could see, and without speaking a word, Audred came and changed the bandages for me. The pity in her expression spoke enough. But the wounds didn't bother me anymore. I could move my hands without debilitating pain, and the scars would only embellish what was already there.

I even completed my yardwork early one afternoon and came back inside to find Audred and Asterra in fine ballgowns, waiting by the front door as Trolaine spoke with the carriage driver outside.

"I thought you were all going to visit with one of Lord Trolaine's friends tonight," I mumbled, but I already knew the truth. There was to be another ball, and its very existence was meant to be kept from me.

They jumped at my presence, then turned faces as red as their hair away from me, their gazes looking anywhere but in my direction.

"It was Father's idea," Asterra whispered, then pretended she didn't even notice me as he returned to the entrance with a glare darkening his face.

"Why do you look so astonished?" he snapped at me.

I didn't bother to dare an answer, schooling my expression.

"Why would you need to know about tonight's ball, hrm?

There's no point, because you wouldn't be going anyway, would you?"

Dred and Terra both flinched at the bite in his words, my stepsisters throwing me cursory glances. I remained stone still apart from the short, panting breaths of subdued anger. Anger that I was getting tired of suppressing.

"You're certainly not the type to be sneaking about, sewing a mockery of a dress to attend without permission. Who knows what a person like that might do? Not you, though, as you've been taught that lesson and are grateful for it."

He watched me expectantly, and I forced breath up my throat in a rough, "Thank you, my lord."

"Girls!" They each went rigid at the word. "You'll be attending the ball without me tonight. I feel my time is better spent here, to make sure our servant keeps to her duties."

They bobbed in unison. "Yes, Father."

He stepped closer to Audred, adjusting her dress, then placing his hands on her shoulders in a firm squeeze. "Be sure to make use of tonight. Without my guidance, it will be more difficult, but you must gain the attention of the prince no matter what."

She blinked rapidly, her eyes unfocused for a moment before nodding. She clutched desperately for Asterra's hand, and they hurried together to the carriage, leaving me alone to face what punishment I dare not even imagine.

A WISH OF ASHES AND GLASS

But Trolaine only eyed me briefly, his moustache twitching, before giving me a list of instructions for chores that would no doubt fill my night and beyond.

I went straight to them, relief only overshadowed with the longing for the ball that passed by as I worked, and for Ara.

She must be wondering what became of me. Is she worried about my injuries? Or angry that I ran away again? She had been right that the statue falling wasn't an accident, and the second attack only proved more that someone was staging these incidents. Why had the king even risked holding a third ball?

I hoped they hadn't caught the fire-breather and placed the blame on him. Even so, that wouldn't make the third ball safe. I was sure he was not involved and had no warning of the explosion; otherwise, why would he risk getting burnt himself?

Whoever was behind the threat was still unidentified. Which meant more people were likely to be hurt, because now the culprit had the opportunity to strike a third time.

What if the person hurt this time was Ara?

There was no chance for me to get to the ball tonight. Trolaine ducked in and out, trailing me around the manor as I scrubbed floors and re-upholstered chairs and darned socks. He didn't stay by my side, as though that were too repulsive to him, but he checked on me so constantly it frayed my nerves and scattered my efforts.

I wasn't getting through the list nearly as fast as I would normally and made mistakes that Trolaine relished to point out.

When he bellowed across the house for me to come to his study, my back already ached, my healing hands felt cracked and raw, and I was tired. So tired of everything.

He stood like a wrathful monster in the center of his study, and the moment I appeared, he boomed, "You lazy, useless vermin!"

I could rouse no defiance, no strength. It was near midnight, and I'd not rested a moment all day. "What have I done?" I asked, my voice forlorn.

"What have you done?" He lashed out and grabbed me by the scruff of the neck, driving me over to the fireplace. A fireplace without its ever-burning fire. Only cold ashes spread across the grate. "Did you plan to leave me cold in here? Hope I succumb to some illness?"

The sight of the burnt-out fire did awaken a scrap of fury in me. There was no real reason this fire needed to burn all day and night. No reason Trolaine's desire that it did needed to add so much to my already heavy burdens. Could he not throw a log on himself?

I stepped out of his hold and snarled, "Perhaps I wouldn't have neglected this one task if you hadn't given me hundreds. You spend me on useless chores as though it is a sport!"

"How dare you speak that way to me!" He grabbed for

my neck again and threw me down into the dead fire. I landed hard on my hands and cried out. A gust of fine ashes filled my lungs. I coughed wretchedly.

I tried to back out of the cloud, but a foot came down heavy on the small of my back, and I heard Trolaine pull something from the rack of fire tools, the harsh scrape of heavy metal.

"Please, please no!" I scrambled in the crumbling, still warm coals but couldn't crawl out from under his boot.

I wasn't prepared when the heavy metal rod came down over my shoulder blades. The blow rattled up my spine, and bolts of pain dizzied me. My face bounced down into the ashes again, and I choked, gulping in the powdery, acid taste.

"You're a pest, a rat, scratching and stealing from those who house you." He brought the poker down across my back again, and I arched in pain, squirming for escape, barely able to breathe. Grit flew into my eyes. "You will learn your place. You will learn that I would do anything for my daughters."

My fist closed around a handful of ash, and wildly, I flung it backward. Trolaine coughed and spluttered, swearing and stepping back, the poker clanging to the floor. I scrambled out of the fireplace and ran. On wobbly, aching legs, I ran, and ran, and didn't ever want to stop.

Sobs clogged my ash-burned throat, and I could barely see. I rushed in a hopeless stumble to my parents' graves, my legs finally giving out as Midnight chimed on the tree, but I did not look up. I could only crush myself to the ground my mother was buried beneath and weep.

I was wrong. I couldn't endure anymore. I couldn't live like this. I couldn't stay here a day longer. I couldn't continue to willingly suffer the brazen cruelty of my stepfather.

When the tree opened for me, its magical door beckoning, I knew what I would do. I pushed myself to my feet and stepped through.

I couldn't even cast my eyes over the gown it gifted me. I had no heart left to see its beauty. I only wished to fly from this place and never return.

When my horse stepped out, clopping its cog-jointed legs to my side, I lashed my arms around its cold neck and hugged it tight. Slipping onto its back, I thought I saw movement in the shadows of the orchard, but we were already galloping away.

I closed my eyes and whispered, "Go. Never stop running."

I didn't want to go to the palace. I wanted to disappear into the night, go anywhere, no matter what fate it brought me, as long as I was gone from this wretched place that was once my home.

I knew my horse, my gown, would both vanish at midnight. That is how everything was for me. Good things never stayed in my life, and I would never be able to cling to happiness for long. It was all destined to vanish from me. And I had already

decorated my skin and heart with more scars than I could bear.

I only opened my eyes when my clockwork companion slowed to a trot. Sitting up in the saddle, I surveyed my surroundings. We were at the palace. The magical horse had taken me right up into the grounds, coming in some back way, avoiding the trailing queue of other guests just visible around the corner.

"No, I don't want to be here. Please take me away. I don't care where. Just take me away." I tried to guide it, to spur it back into movement, but my horse refused, instead walking me closer to a terrace and lowering down onto its knees. I slumped from its back onto the damp grass and remained there as my clockwork steed abandoned me.

I curled numbly on the ground, glittering skirts pooling around me like a sea of rippling tears. I didn't move as the night air chilled my bare arms. The hot marks where Trolaine had struck me cooled, and my muscles stiffened, locked and exhausted. My tears had almost, almost slowed when I heard a sound.

"El?" The voice was timid, searching.

Ara held rose-red slippers in one hand as she approached, barefooted over the dewy grass. Matching vermillion silk clung to her curves, sewn into the most delicate and intricate folds, accented with jewels, and trailing behind her like a spill of fresh blood. Her shoulders were bare, except for where her dark hair, free and loose, tumbled in neat curls over them.

Taking in my face, in its display of naked grief, she broke into a run.

Her hands went to my face, wiping my cheeks. Her breath came fast, and her eyes flashed furiously. "What has happened?"

I could only stare at her, the incongruity of her glamorous gown with the muscled arms of a sword fighter somehow made her more alluring.

I touched a hand to the silk as though testing it was real. "You … You're …"

"Devastatingly beautiful? Yes, I know."

"… wearing a *dress*."

Ara quirked a smile at me, but her eyes were still intense and her brows low. "Come, come inside with me, and tell me what has hurt you so I can hurt it back."

I looked up at the palace, the ballroom, the potential for more pain. "I can't. I can't go in. I'm scared … If there's another attack—"

"Then I'll protect you." She reached for my hands, then instead reached farther, clasping me around the elbows. Only then did I see my burns and scars were covered in long, shimmering gloves of a blue so pale it could be white. She pulled to lift me to my feet, but I strained against her, still unwilling to move.

"Please," she whispered. "Stay by my side, and no one

will dare to hurt you."

"Why?" I breathed in return, meaning so many questions in that one word. Why wouldn't anyone hurt me? Why was she here with me? Why did she care? Why me?

But she only answered one of my questions. She sighed, long and low. "Because I'm Princess Miara."

TEN

ARA—PRINCESS MIARA—gently led me to the terrace. Warm light spilled out through the windows onto the paving. Rose bushes, potted in massive urns, rustled in the breeze, blending with the muffled music of the ball going on without us. My eyes felt raw and hot from the earlier flow of tears now dried on my cheeks.

"I'm so sorry for keeping the truth from you." Ara guided me by an elbow to a marble bench and knelt in front of me as I sat. "But it had felt nice not to be judged based on my royal blood for once."

I only stared at her, open-mouthed, unsure what to think. Ara was a princess?

She glanced up at me, then away quickly, her full lips

twisting as she slipped her shoes back on. "Also, frankly, I already have *so much* going for me both in looks and my fine wit, that when people also know I'm a princess, it's simply overwhelming."

It was indeed a little overwhelming. *Princess Miara.* I wasn't sure if I should be bowing, addressing her by her title, or groveling for forgiveness for my behavior. My cheeks heated at the memory of the way I spoke to her when we first met. But I looked into her golden eyes, and she was still *Ara* and asked nothing from me for her status.

I returned a weak smirk. "You're also top-notch at modesty."

"Oh yes, the absolute best."

Shocking myself, a snort giggled from my mouth. "You're a little bit ridiculous too."

"Anything to see you smile. Now, let me see your hands."

She reached for my gloves, peeling them down slowly with the lightest touch. "Are the burns still hurting you?"

I shrugged. I couldn't feel much at that moment other than her all-consuming, tender touch, and the shivers that it sent shooting through my body.

"We could have seen to them here. Why did you leave?"

"I didn't want to trouble anyone. It wasn't as bad as it seemed, really."

Ara huffed. "I feel like I've been hearing that a lot lately." With the gloves removed, she cautiously inspected my hands, her painstakingly gentle touch sending thrills up my arms that made me tremble again. "They do seem to have healed well. I could have sworn they were worse … But I'm glad they aren't."

The lesser extent of my injuries hadn't smoothed the deep wrinkle that set between Ara's brows. I pulled my gloves back on, marveling at the sheer, sparkling fabric that glimmered like it had stars trapped between the fibers, and attempted to move the conversation away from my injuries, lest in weakness I speak of the aching welts across my shoulders.

"You seem troubled."

"There is a lot to be troubled about," Ara agreed.

"The attacks on the king?" I prompted.

"Maybe not the king. There have been so many rumors spreading now, including that I am the one attempting to kill my brother. Because as the eldest, I would be heir to the throne if he were gone, so I have most to gain. And what with how I am"—her voice changed, becoming mocking—"too headstrong, too masculine, too ambitious! What princess would want to be so involved in the military without some other motive?"

She rose to standing, her dress clinging to her curves like a second skin. She was magnificent in her height, and I wondered how I could ever have thought she was anything other than royalty with that fierce regal presence.

"Hence the gown." She sighed and swished her skirts primly. "My effort to smooth things over, behave as they think I should. Be the good princess."

I stood in a hurry in front of her, driven up by indignation. "But of course you wouldn't be behind the attacks. You seem to be the only person trying to discover who really is!"

Ara smiled, but it didn't reach her eyes. She wiped my cheek again, as though brushing away the ghosts of my tears. "But it feels like there might be some truth in the rumors. That maybe the attacks aren't aimed at the king, but perhaps my brother. There is something so odd about them. I must find out who is setting them up and why so I can clear my own name."

"I'll do whatever I can to help."

Rising strains of string music breached the palace walls, reminding me of a different world that played out inside. A prince trying to find his bride. All the eligible women of the kingdom hoping it would be them. A world that seemed so distant now that I had almost forgotten its existence. What did any of that matter when all I wanted was right here before me now?

Ara listened for a moment too, then reached for my hand. "Dance with me?"

A soft tremor quietened her voice, and her gaze was solemn and intense as she awaited my answer.

"You want to dance?" I rested my fingers into hers, breathless, and stepped closer, my body answering the invitation as my mind still grappled with the concept. *The princess wants to dance ... with me?*

She nodded and led me inside, toward the ballroom, her grip featherlight on my sore fingers. "It will give us a good way to move around and survey the ballroom. Plus, I'll be seen as doing my princessly duties and keeping my nose clean. Although one would think I'd had enough dancing in my lifetime."

"Oh, of course." I shouldn't have thought a princess would want to dance with me, if not only as a ruse to keep up our investigation. I must have imagined the tremor in her voice, or at least imagined the wrong reason for it.

Ara rambled as we moved. "Why the king has even allowed another ball, it beggars belief. There are simply so many strangers present, so much risk. For what, so my terrible brother can find a bride? As though he would find that difficult at all when he's grown and ready."

"He does look quite young still."

"Acts it, too. Even after the first ball, even before I knew for sure, I did what I could to increase security, but still there was another attack. I managed to track down that fire-breather the next day—"

"You did?" My voice raised in an unpleasant squeak, and

I almost tripped down the smooth, carpeted hallway.

Ara nodded, turning back slightly to show a face twisted in confusion. "A simple man. With a family. Didn't seem the type to attempt treason for love or money and couldn't answer any questions. Plainly bewildered by the whole experience. I let him go. I only hope I was right to."

I breathed a sigh of relief, happy in the knowledge that the fire-breather was safe, and so, it seemed was my secret. We strode out onto the floor as the music swelled.

"I'm sure you were right. Though I've known you briefly, I've only seen you act with a logic that is made stronger by being tempered with compassion. If those aren't the qualities of a princess, then I don't know what are, but regardless, they are the qualities of the very best of any human."

Looking into my eyes in a way that made my legs feel as stable as water, Ara led me into a waltz.

We weren't the only women dancing together, as there were so many more women than men at the ball. Ara held her hand open and let me rest mine into it in the way I found comfortable. Even with her second hand on my waist, she barely touched the fabric of my dress, as though frightened to hurt me without reason, as though I was made of glass.

What had been made of glass, though—I was shocked to see now grief no longer clouded my eyes—were my slippers. They seemed cut from diamond, sparkling when they peeked out from beneath my skirts.

And the gown … I may as well have been dipped in starlight, bathed in a galaxy and come out glistening. I had never seen such fabric and couldn't name it, but it shot rainbows of scintillating light with every motion. It clung to my neck, shoulders, and down my chest like a second skin, then spilled in a radiant waterfall around me.

And here I was, dancing with a princess.

I should have been looking around, trying to spot any suspicious behavior, any clue that could help solve the case, or even to spot my stepsisters and keep out of their view, but I couldn't take my eyes off Ara, and her eyes remained locked on me.

"Tell me, please, who are you?" Ara's voice came out husky, almost lost beneath the music and dancing footsteps.

What could I say? She knew I was a servant, but the full reality of my situation felt so much more shameful.

Could she keep me from harm if she knew the truth? She was the princess. If she wished, could she remove Trolaine's hold over me? Did I dare ask that of her?

My hesitation crushed her expression. "I am begging you, El. I'm so frightened. The fact that you can't tell me, that there's clearly some secret or danger that is hurting you and holding your truth hostage, is destroying me with worry." Ara's hand on my waist curled further around me, softly drawing me into her. My starry chest pressed against hers. "These nights together, these events, can't continue indefinitely. And if they end, if this is the last—"

A hand landed on my shoulder, and our dance stopped. We both turned to see Prince Creston there, smiling under sly eyes. "Miara, dear sister, might I cut in?"

She grunted. "Not *now*, Cres!"

"Excuse me?" he said, imperious.

Ara dropped her eyes and winced. "I'm sorry." Clearly not, she continued, "But you have every woman in the kingdom here waiting to dance with you, why do you need my time?"

"Oh, not you." He bowed slightly, offering me his hand. "Shall we?"

"Absolutely not," Ara said.

Creston raised his eyebrows as though raising an executioner's axe and opened his mouth, but I rushed to speak first. "It's fine, I'd be pleased to dance with the prince. I don't want to make a scene."

"You don't have to," Ara pleaded, unwilling to let go of my hand.

"I'm afraid she does," Creston said, dragging me away.

"It's all right." Her fingertips trailed out of mine, and I held her gaze for as long as I could as Creston drew me abruptly into our waltzing pose. He swirled us away from Ara into the other dancers. I turned my head, seeking Ara as she disappeared.

There was nothing gentle in Creston's touch, or his interrogation. "Who are you to my sister?"

I snapped my attention to him and gaped. Who was I to Ara? I wanted to be so much, but she didn't even know who I truly was. I had only just found out who *she* truly was.

Eyes lowered, I said, "I barely know her."

"Then why does she defend you? What is your value?"

My spine straightened and I pressed my mouth into a thin line. Assuming me some object or tool that could be evaluated for worth felt far too close to Trolaine's approach to the women in his life.

Instead of answering the question as to *my value*, I returned a question of my own. "Is it not in A—*Miara's* nature to defend, regardless of who requires it and their value?"

He snorted. "I thought you barely knew her."

"We met at the first ball."

"Not before? Not in time to make plans, put them into action?"

I pursed my lips. "Honestly, I think she was too inebriated at the first ball to have put much of anything into action."

That left Creston's mouth hanging. His shoulder's dropped from their tense height, and he pouted a dreadful teenage pout. This close, I could see his eyes were the same color as Ara's.

I softened. "You must be viewing the world from a depth

of great sadness to believe your sister would want to kill you."

Creston looked for a moment as though he choked.

But now that I could see it, the sorrow hiding behind his hard eyes and curled lip, it was impossible to dismiss. "What could make a prince so sad? Look around us. Half the kingdom is here to make you happy."

He barked a harsh laugh. "Make me happy? They are here to win a competition, and I'm nothing but the prize. I despise this whole affair. I am a trophy hung out above the fighting ring. My own life isn't mine."

My heart filled my throat, and I could only gape at him for a long moment. With every sincerity, I whispered, "I'm so sorry. I hope you are able to take control of your path."

His expression darkened, shifted, grew confused. He gripped my hand tightly, crushing my healing burns. I cried out.

"That's it, you're done." Ara appeared by our side and wrenched him off me, shoving him back by the shoulder. Gasps went up all around.

Creston righted himself and straightened his coat. "We're not done until *I* say we are."

"Then say you are before I knock you flat on your back like you know I can."

Creston spluttered, but Ara didn't wait for him to spit out a reply. She took me at her side and walked me away. A clearing had formed around us as the scandalized crowd

watched the drama unfold, other dancers moving back to let us pass.

Only one woman saw the opportunity and acted fast. Audred headed straight for the prince and his empty space for a dance partner, her expression a forced smile laced with determination.

"Ara!" he bellowed, but the princess didn't slow. I turned back, horrified by the anger I saw on his face and what it could lead to. Then I had something else to fear.

A twang. A scream. Then movement. The sky seemed to fall.

An enormous chandelier plummeted down into the open space between us and the prince. Without even seconds to spare, Creston dived away, skidding on his side.

Ara drew me fast toward her, and a wall of black and gold appeared, guards, forming a barrier between us and a hailstorm of shattering crystal.

Shards jingled across the floor like a million tiny bells, and as they stilled, a more terrifying danger appeared as Creston scrambled to his feet, stormed across the crackling glass, drew a sword from a guard's scabbard, and pointed it at Ara.

"Traitor!"

Eleven

ARA REMAINED STILL, keeping me shielded behind her. Her voice was low and dangerous. "Don't be a fool, Cres. I didn't do this."

Prince Creston waved his sword, gesturing to the guards at our sides. "You've turned the guards from their duty! Look at them, more loyal to you than the heir himself! They should have been protecting me."

"They weren't close enough. They would have been under the chandelier itself if they tried to get to you."

"Or were they in on the plot to kill me, too? You and your co-conspirator there, ending our dance just in time?" He jabbed his sword directly at me.

Ara bowed her head and sighed. She whispered back to

me, "You had better leave."

"But—"

Ara reached across to the closest guard and took his sword. "Get out of here, quickly."

I stumbled back, crystal shards slipping under my heels, and pushed into the crowd to distance myself from Ara and her brother. I did not want to leave her side but felt it best to do as she said rather than deny the princess and add to the scene.

So I made my escape through the throng. Some of the bystanders stared and muttered at me, but most kept their eyes glued to the prince and princess.

I heard Creston snarl from behind me. "Now she shows her true colors."

In response, Ara's voice drifted through the room, calm and clear. "No, brother. Now I will defend myself until you are thinking clearly. If I wanted you dead, how long do you think you'll last once swords start swinging?"

The prince howled in fury, and there was a bright clang of sword meeting sword.

No. I wanted to go back, make it stop, protect Ara, but how could I? I was no fighter, and my presence only seemed to make matters worse. Ara drew a sword on her own brother, the crown prince, to defend me. I had made *everything* worse.

Still, I had almost given in to the urge to turn around,

to run back and try to make them stop fighting each other, when toward the back of the crowd I was shocked to a stop. A body lay in my path, looking like a pile of discarded fabric. I ducked down beside her, surrounded by the press of wide skirts and soft frills.

She didn't even react to me. The woman was curled on her side, shivering visibly, and holding bloody hands in front of her face.

A face I knew too well. *Audred.*

Her eyes were so wide the whites showed around every side of her irises, and her lips moved and muttered between panting breaths.

I remembered seeing my stepsister approach the prince right before the chandelier came down. A neat slice cut straight down her right cheekbone to the corner of her lips. Deep enough that the edges were curling outward as the injury swelled, spilling vivid crimson blood down her face.

Her eyes flicked suddenly to me. Wild with confusion, pain, and overwhelming terror. "I'm cut, I'm cut! My face … will it scar? It will, it will. Oh, I am ruined. I will be nothing. What can I be for Father if I'm ugly? What can I be to anyone? I will be nothing. I will be worth nothing." Every word was a frantic sob that tumbled from her mouth like heavy stones, and her eyes rolled, addled with distress, red, and sheened with tears.

"Oh, Audred." My heart hurt wretchedly for her. I pressed a hand to her uncut cheek, and her twitching gaze turned back to me. I couldn't tell if she knew who I was, or if she was too panicked to care about anything other than herself. Her expression only showed blind fear.

"Nothing, nothing," she chanted as though locked in a loop.

Another single clash of swords echoed through the room. Creston and Ara's voices were lost under the gasp of the crowd. Everything felt broken, spoiled, and I knew what I had to do I would have no coming back from. But how could I not? What was one more scar, for me?

I leaned in close. "You'll never be nothing to me. You will always be my tormentor ... and my comforter. You have shown me as much kindness as you've dared, and I don't blame you for not showing more while protecting yourself. You're my sister, and I love you."

Her gaze settled, stilled, locked onto mine as the wound on her cheek closed. A heavy recognition filled her eyes, as though she was seeing me for the very first time.

Her mouth opened wide in a silent wail as she looked to my cheek. Blood ran down my face and dripped onto Audred's dress where it bloomed red.

The wound stung like the crack of a cane. A hot, crushing ache also hit my ankle, the tendons tearing as though I'd twisted it. But it must have come from Audred, too. Perhaps it was why she lay fallen here, I realized dimly through the pain.

Neither the cut cheek nor sprained ankle were as bad as the lashings I still felt across my back, the still healing burns, the torn shoulder, the bruised thigh, the aching and scratched fingers from the creatures I saved from traps even that morning.

What hurt and worried me far more was that Audred now knew my secret.

"Her! Get her!" a voice snapped.

I turned my head toward it and saw the king staring through a gap at me, directing guards our way. The chill of fear spiked up my spine, and I scrambled to my feet, then almost fell again with my first step.

But pain, I could endure. With teeth set hard together, I lunged into a hobbled dash, hoping I hadn't tested myself too far and found my limits. Shockwaves shot up my body with every step, making me nauseous as a cold sweat broke over me. I could hardly see through my tears as I pushed out the nearest clear doorway and tried to get my bearings.

I wasn't far from the terrace where I had arrived. I turned that way, lifting my skirts from my feet as I ran. I pushed around a corner, out to the terrace, finding shelter behind one of the huge urns that held rose bushes as a team of soldiers stormed by. I had to press myself in so close that the thorny vines tangled into my hair, caught on the soft skin of my ears and neck.

I stood there, back pressed to the cold marble, leaves bobbing around me in the wind, as I caught my breath.

From somewhere within the castle, a chime rang.

My eyes went wide. What was the time? It couldn't be midnight yet. Down the steps from the terrace, standing on the grounds, my clockwork horse snorted and fretted. A second chime clanged.

No, no no no.

I flew down the stairs, crooked and tumbling. My weak ankle twisted, and the glass shoe slipped off that foot, left behind with no time to consider collecting it.

The third bell rang. I threw myself onto my steed's back, holding tight.

Fourth bell. We rode. Furious, unfettered, a blur of ribbons, cogs, and starry fabric through the dark swath of night.

We were too far from the palace to hear the rest of the bells chime, but I counted them out in my mind.

Fifth. Sixth. Seventh. Eighth. Ninth. Tenth.

We leapt over the garden wall, breaking through the tree line of the forest.

Eleventh. Twelfth.

I wondered for a second whether it hadn't been midnight yet after all. Then the support went out from underneath me, as though I rode on nothing but air.

A WISH OF ASHES AND GLASS

I fell in a clatter. Pieces of cloth, broken porcelain, buttons, and copper wheels smashed to the ground with me.

Fabric tore, and wind whipped all around me. My knees and elbows scraped as I rolled to a stop. I cried out and laid there surrounded by the debris of my clockwork horse as the pain became too much. I wheezed air back into winded lungs and wiped dirt from my cheeks, every part of me aching.

Rolling onto my side, I stared in horrified heartbreak at what had become of my beautiful horse. It had fallen into pieces. Shattered around me like shards of my broken dreams. Whatever magic had brought it to life was gone.

Could it ever come to life again, having not reached the tree in time? Perhaps later, I could collect all the pieces and return them to the tree in the hope that it could be revived. But for now, I could barely lift myself. I reached out and touched the cog that had once been the horse's cheek I'd kissed.

"I'm so sorry," I sobbed.

My gown was also gone, my body back in my ragged servant's dress, my dirty hair tucked under an old scarf. I pulled the scarf off and used it to scrub the tears from my eyes. Everything had gone so wrong.

Dull, cold heaviness formed in my chest. I had to go home. I knew doing so would mean facing Trolaine's wrath for our earlier encounter, but now that Audred knew my secret, I had to return and convince her to keep it for me.

No one else could know what I was capable of.

I limped the rest of the way through the woods, my mind echoing with the clash of swords and worry for Ara.

I had failed her so completely. When we danced, I had been so caught up in my hopeless feelings that I didn't have a chance of spotting who really caused the accidents. I hadn't helped Ara at all, too absorbed in her attention, a desire for her affection that I had no right to wish for.

I'd only made things worse, making Ara feel responsible for my care in my pitiable state, causing her to break off my dance with the prince at the wrong moment.

Reaching the edge of our property, the orchard came into view. In amongst the flowering oranges and pears, my treasure tree shimmered in the moonlight, and a dark figure stood before it.

Lord Trolaine waited for me there, an axe dangling from one hand.

His eyes gleamed as they took me in. "There you are. What wicked scheme did you enact tonight, witch?"

Even had I known what to say, or dared to say anything, I couldn't. My throat was too tightly clogged with fear.

"Don't play ignorant. I saw you casting spells to disguise your identity and ride through time itself. I know now that you're the mystery woman who fled the first and second ball after the dangerous attacks. Are you so jealous of my

daughters that you go to these extremes to block their road to greatness? That you would try to kill the prince himself rather than let them have him?"

"No!" I found my voice again. "Of course not. I never—"

"How do you explain this behavior? Sneaking around, lashing out against my orders, using your dark magic to sabotage my daughters' chances." He hefted the axe into a swinging position.

"That's not—"

"I saw your burns. I know you caused that explosion. You're the one behind the attacks, behind trying to kill the prince. Or were you trying to make my daughters scarred and ugly like you? Either way, you'll never touch them. I'll never give you a chance to harm them ever again."

The axe swung. *Thunk.* The treasure tree shook.

"No! Please!" I dashed forward.

Trolaine wrenched the axe from the tree and cracked the butt of the handle into my ribcage.

I heaved, falling backward onto the ground. My head cracked against a gravestone. My vision dripped with inky swirls.

He swung again. Buttons and pebbles rained down around us.

I tried to move, but my body wasn't responding. Too worn, too abused to continue listening to my commands. I could only lie there and stare as Trolaine struck my treasure tree over and over with his axe.

"Once this cursed junk is destroyed, your source of wicked power will be gone." The tree shook as he hit it again.

The clock lurched out of the fork, hung from a single wire, then toppled down and smashed on the ground. Cogs and sea glass jingled as they shook from branches. My mind faded in and out of darkness, desperately trying to hold on so I could get up and stop him.

Then, a horrible crackling, splitting sound came from the old, twisted trunk.

He swung again, and the canopy leaned, swaying to one side. Wood snapped. My breath caught. The weight of the tree pushed past its center of gravity and came down in a rush, leaves swishing and roaring as it hit the ground like thunder. Treasures and trinkets jangled like hail.

My face scrunched as pain and grief engulfed me. I felt torn open to the core as surely as if the axe had been buried in my chest. I had passed the limits of what I could endure and had nothing left. I was broken. Everything was broken. Everything gone.

Trolaine stood over me, silhouetted by the moon. "All your evil plotting has failed. You will now be the cause of what you tried to end. Because I should no doubt claim betrothal to the prince for one of my daughters as reward for turning in the witch who attacked the royal family."

TWELVE

MY NIGHT WAS spent bound and gagged, curled in pain on the cold cellar floor.

And it was in the same state that I was delivered to the palace.

Trolaine dragged me from the carriage, and once he explained the reason for his presence, a troop of guards escorted us immediately to the king.

None of the guards were Ara, and in my pain-blurred mind, I had to remind myself that she was Princess Miara and that her fate may match mine. What punishment had she earned for clashing swords with the prince?

One guard was familiar, though. Tobin. He glanced at me once but showed no sign of recognition. I kept my gaze on him, pleading and desperate, but I couldn't get Tobin's attention to ask what happened to Ara.

The rope that bound my wrists was so tight I'd lost feeling in my fingers, and my hair scarf had been tied roughly between my teeth, so even if I did find the opportunity to speak with the young guard, I would not be able to. I limped, hindered by my injured ankle, being pushed along to keep pace beside Trolaine.

An announcement was made up ahead and gilded double doors swung wide. The guards marched and I stumbled into formal chambers where the king reclined on a lounge, with his advisor, Hareth, standing close behind.

The atmosphere was dark and oppressive. Cloying scents puffed from censers hanging in every corner. Heavy velvet curtains shielded the smokey shadows from being pierced by bright morning rays. The room was as gloomy as the heavy blanket of sadness that shrouded my heart.

King Othon coughed wretchedly for two solid minutes before wiping his mouth on a handkerchief and turning his attention to us. He leaned forward shakily, bloodshot eyes narrowed at our appearance. His arms and shoulders were wasted away, boney and crooked.

Trolaine bowed down into a kneeling position. "Your Majesty. I am your humble servant, and I've discovered the one who has plotted against you and your kin."

King Othon clicked a finger. Hareth came to my side

and dragged me by an elbow to kneel at the king's feet. Then he picked up a lamp and brought it over, holding it up near my face. I flinched at the sudden light, blinking back tears.

The king leaned in close. His breath smelled like bad milk laced with the coppery tang of blood.

"Yes, that's her, the one we were after. You've served me well," Othon paused and lifted his chin to my stepfather.

"Lord Trolaine, Your Majesty." He got to his feet, and his chest heaved with breaths of excitement. "I am so pleased to have brought you something so valuable."

Othon tutted and leaned back into the lounge again as though preparing to fall asleep but kept his gaze on me. "Valuable. Yes, yes. You want some reward, of course?"

Trolaine wrung his hands together. "I wouldn't dare ask … but in exchange for my gift to you, if you would offer your consideration for one of my beautiful daughters to be Prince Creston's bride, I would be honored. If he has still not yet found one after the great expense of three grand balls dedicated to that cause."

King Othon smiled at me, huffing a laugh that reminded me so much of Ara. "I see. You want to trade. This girl for a royal son-in-law. Very well, it does make for a tidy solution. Your daughter can marry Creston."

Trolaine bobbed three grateful bows in a row, beaming beneath his red moustache. "I have two daughters, Your

Majesty, that you may consider. The first is lovely as a spring morning and perfectly obedient. A lady with many virtues. The second is just as lovely and closer to the prince's age—"

"I really don't care. You can choose. Hareth will sort out all the details," Othon muttered. He waved to the guards, and they took it as their cue to escort Trolaine away. But still the king's eyes remained locked on me.

"Your Majesty, thank you. Thank you. You will be so pleased …" Trolaine's voice trailed off, and the doors closed behind him, leaving me, King Othon, and Hareth alone in the room.

King Othon coughed roughly again, then offered me a smile that wobbled around blood-stained lips. "Hareth, come untie this child."

The advisor moved swiftly to my side and pulled the scarf down from my mouth. He lifted me back to my feet and began working on the knots binding my hands.

I took a deep breath, steadied my aching body, and once my hands were free, I dropped myself down before the king, bowing low. "Your Majesty, I had no part in the attacks, I swear to you. Nor did Princess Miara. Please don't punish her for what she didn't do."

King Othon chuckled roughly, snorting through his nose. I lifted my forehead from the floor, and he waved me back to my feet. Hareth remained at my side, helping me up again with a gentle hand.

"Oh, I know, child, I know. Of course you didn't execute the attacks." King Othon's eyes glimmered in the dim light, a warm, bright brown. Not quite the gold of Ara's and without their gentleness. There was something hard in his gaze that frightened me, despite his words bringing relief.

Then he added, "It was Hareth who set those events into action."

I stepped back from the man, expecting him to rage at the accusation, expecting guards to burst in and throw him to the floor and drag him to the dungeons. But instead, he bowed neatly to Kind Othon as though he'd been bestowed an honor.

"Under my orders," King Othon explained.

I looked between the two of them, my skin tingling all over. "What? Why?"

Had he been trying to kill his own son? It didn't make sense. Ara had been right that nothing seemed to add up about the attacks. Who they targeted, why they failed. But maybe they didn't target anyone for death. Maybe they didn't fail. I found myself shaking violently, fearful of the dark revelation looming toward me.

"The events were a farce. They were never held for the purpose of finding my useless son a bride."

"Why then?" My voice was tiny, my mind already starting

to see an answer forming that I didn't want to hear.

King Othon smiled with deep satisfaction. "I saw you, on the street that day, a kindhearted girl helping the stupid child who went under my carriage. Such a show of magic! And I thought, what else would that girl do? What else *could* she do? Unfortunately, you were gone before my guards were able to round you up."

Another fit of coughs wracked the king's body. I looked about, to the windows, the door, for any chance of escape, but Hareth wrapped a hand tight around one of my arms.

Othon wheezed. "So, Hareth and I came up with the idea of these grand dances every woman in the right age range would be lured to with the bribe of winning the prince's hand. We knew you surely weren't already married, filthy wretch that you were. Then all that was needed was some accident, somebody injured—anybody, it didn't matter—in the hopes you'd act again on your kind heart, and we would discover you."

The warmth of life seemed to flee my body, leaving me frozen and numb. All of it, all the events, the attacks, it had all been set up to find *me*.

Each "accident" had always occurred near the king but not close enough to ever threaten him. Just close enough that he could observe the results. I'd gotten lucky managing to sneak away one way or another, causing Othon to hold another event, to put more innocent people under threat to draw me out.

And it was clear why.

He wiped blood from his lips and beckoned to me. "Come, kind heart, come and heal your king. With you by my side, I can be healthy and rule for many, many years yet and never have to hand my throne to my failure of an heir."

My feet didn't move. I stared in horror at the man hunched on the lounge, body so wasted and ashen it looked one step away from death. This man, who had lied to his whole kingdom and caused so much heartache and danger for the goal of maintaining his own life. I knew my vow, but I couldn't bring myself to wish this man's life extended so he could continue to rule with such selfish cruelty. I could not let this wretched man be the death of me.

I found my voice and lifted my chin. "No. I won't."

Hareth tightened his grip and dragged me right in front of the king.

Othon nodded almost sadly. "You will, though. You will take this illness from me, and you will take every hurt or ailment to assault my body from here on out. Or Miara will be the one to suffer instead. Yes, I know you're fond of her, and she clearly is of you, too. She's out there right now, searching the kingdom for the woman who left the glass slipper behind. You will heal me, or it is her life ended instead."

My heart seemed to shudder against my ribs, aching with every shaky thump. "But she's your daughter."

Old blood crusted the sides of Othon's lips, and he stared at me with eyes like knives. "I have so many daughters, after all. I shouldn't miss one."

My shoulder's slumped, and I nodded dully. With a body already suffering beyond its limits, I reached for the king's hand and opened my magic with intent.

Taking the king's illness was a slow kind of pain at first. Like having poison mixed into my blood drip by drip.

Then my vision paled, like staring through watery milk, and tremors of agony jolted along my bones, wilting my muscles. A crushing pressure filled my lungs, and my body jerked uncontrollably, crumpling to the floor, coughing and spluttering. Hideous spurts of blood gushed from my nose and lips. Every breath felt like the act of a torturer who'd taken their craft too far.

Two figures, gray blobs, loomed over me as I twitched and curled in anguish on the floor. Othon and Hareth. Uncrumpled, Othon seemed huge. Taller than Ara. Far, far bigger than me.

The king raised his arms up before his face. "I feel amazing. This is a miracle. This is what we've sought so long."

"It is as you deserve, Your Majesty," Hareth replied.

"We must make plans. What I could do with this renewed strength! But first, hide her away in the side chamber. Make

sure she stays quiet. We have another meeting shortly."

I couldn't fight the hands that pulled the scarf back over my mouth, that wrapped the rope back around my wrists. I was dragged across the floor, a convulsing, bloody mess, blind with pain. A door closed. I huddled in darkness on a cold, unyielding floor. As my consciousness tried to let go, tried to take me from this agony into the solace of oblivion, a deeper fear held me in its grip.

As I had healed the king, taken his symptoms, I had felt a deeper sickness, tangled within the man's very bones, that wouldn't shift. The cause of his blight remained in him.

And when his symptoms returned, what would that mean for me? If I could not heal him completely, what would that mean for Ara?

Thirteen

VOICES … TALKING. YELLING. Footsteps. Silence again. I cried for a while. I lay in a stupor, dry heaving around the scarf in my mouth in an endless rhythm.

Then a voice I recognized hummed to my ears.

"Creston? Where's Father?"

Low mumbles resolved into words. "—missed him. He has announced to me my betrothal, then left to see to—" Then they became blurred sounds again.

Holding my breath, I fought to still my body, wrench control back from the wracking convulsions pulsing through me. Hearing Ara's voice, knowing she was safe, gave me strength. I tried to call out.

The cracked whisper of my voice didn't pass audibly

through the scarf gagging me, let alone through the door that stood between us.

It was so hard to even lift my head, push air through my throat. In return for my efforts, I choked on a clot of blood and almost passed out. But I held tight to consciousness, fighting the brume of pain, and the voices came through clearer.

"With no more dances, you'll have to change your plans to murder me."

"By the sun, Cres, I had no part in the attacks and never wanted you dead. If you still believe that, you're dafter than I'd even thought. All I want right now is to find El. I'm worried about her safety. I was hoping the king would grant me use of some soldiers to help my search."

"You're the daft one if you think he'll grant you swords to your cause when you're still a suspect."

"Then I'll keep searching on my own." Footsteps. Ara marching away.

"Why?" Creston called out loudly. "Why now, after all this time, would you turn your back on your ambitions for one person? Now, when the kingdom could so easily be yours?"

The footsteps stopped, then came back.

Ara's voice was flat and heavy. "No matter the hate we've often shared between us, you are my family, and I know my duty. I would never take the throne from you and would, and *have,* fought to protect others from doing so, too. I know the

crown will never be mine."

A pause, a deep breath. "It will never be mine, either."

"Cres?"

"I know. It couldn't have been you trying to kill me. You've never taken on a task in your life that wasn't completed with efficiency and precision. I won't seek punishment against you for drawing against me, as I drew on you in sheer foolishness. Nor will I seek to take the throne."

Soft words, muffled through timber and pain.

"No, I never wanted to be king. I was never able to rouse the passion or skill for the role. I simply wasn't allowed any alternative. You can imagine my jealousy of you. Always able to master every kingly pursuit effortlessly—"

"Never effortlessly. Never."

"And I hated you, how you could want something, anything, with such fervor, even when that goal would never be in your reach. And everyone would point to you and say, 'That is how a king behaves!' But not her. It can't be her. It must be *you*. No matter what either of us wanted."

"Cres. I'm so sorry. I never wanted to make you feel less than you are. Than you should be." There was shuffling, the gentle thud of bodies meeting in a firm embrace. Ara's voice was thick, muffled. "You're enough of a whiney brat already."

Soft laughter came from them. "You know, I made your mystery woman dance with me because I thought maybe she was the one thing you wanted that I could take. And even there, I was wrong. I hope you find her."

"I will search every part of this kingdom until I do."

My breathing came a little easier. Still stifled by blood crusted nostrils and the scarf in my mouth, but smoother, less full of blades. My body had stilled, and the pain eased. It was almost as though I could sense Ara's closeness, that her simple presence nearby brought me peace.

Knowing that she was looking for me, that she cared enough to search for me, tightened my chest with a deep heartache and sense of panic. Because all her searching of the kingdom would do nothing but take her away from me, because I was here. I was right *here*.

I wanted to scream out to her. With a strained effort, I rubbed my cheek against the bare stone floor, dragging at the gag.

Creston spoke again. "I won't be here when you get back. I'm leaving. I don't want my marriage, or my future, arranged for me. I only want to be free of it all."

"What? You can't. Where would you go?"

"Wherever I want. I've bemoaned my lack of freedom like, well, like a whiney brat, all these years, when I always had the choice to change my path. I don't think the world out there will be too cruel to me, nor will I be missed here."

"You will be. Don't be too hasty, Cres." Ara's voice

sounded muffled again. There was a patting sound, then footsteps.

"Good luck, Ara."

My cheek heated and stung, grazed on the floor as I grew frantic. The corner of a tile caught the gag, and the scarf pulled down, freeing my mouth.

"Ara!" I bellowed, but my voice emerged as a hoarse croak, not loud enough for her to hear. I coughed, then rolled onto my front and crawled my legs under me so I could sit up. "Ara!"

The room I'd been left in was dark, and my vision glazed, but I stood and tumbled to where I thought the door was. I smacked into timber, and it rattled. Turning around, I felt with my bound hands, fingers grasping blindly. It felt like an eternity before I found the handle.

It turned. It had been left unlocked. I stumbled out into the room to find it empty.

"Ara?" I cried again, hoping she'd return. I hobbled across the floor.

Bodies approached at a fast march until they filled my blurred vision. Dark uniforms, led by a man renewed to his full, regal height. I tried to turn, to run the other way, but I was caught up by guards and hoisted up by my elbows. My gag I'd worked so hard to remove was replaced in a second.

"Bring her," the king commanded. "The traitor's final

accommodations have been prepared."

They marched, and I was dragged down a corridor and through a study lined with books. The king stopped beside a grandfather clock flanked by shelves and pulled a chain from around his neck. Something short and straight dangled on the end, glinting in the candlelight. He removed a book from the shelf and pressed the metal rod into a hidden hole.

With a click, the bookcase swung open, and I was shoved roughly into the chamber behind it and dropped there on the ground.

The guards backed away as I scrambled upright, seeking them with pleading eyes. I sobbed beneath my gag, and the king looked down at me, a heavy sympathy dragging his features down.

"I know. I know it hurts. And this will be a hard place with little comfort to be suffering such pain." He gestured to the rough walls, the lack of furniture or windows, nothing but hard stone on every side. "But we have to make sure you can never, ever get away."

FOURTEEN

KING OTHON CAME to me every day. At least, it seemed that way. My hidden cell had no light, but I could hear the bell of the nearby clock, dull and distant through stone wall. Often, I was too ill, too senseless to listen for it, but when I did, every second time it chimed twelve, Othon would appear.

He'd been angry with me the first time. Angry my magic hadn't lasted, as though I should be able to control it better, and I was trying to deceive him. He'd grasped my wrists roughly and pressed my hands against his cheeks, yelling for me to cure him. And I tried. I really tried.

But the next day, he was back, weakened again, requiring healing again.

He'd only kept me at first because my valuable gift might

have been needed at some unknown moment in the future. But when it became clear I would be needed every day to maintain Othon's health, greater care was taken to preserve me.

Blankets had been tucked around me at some point, a cushion propped under my head. A bucket left in the corner. Somebody, Hareth most likely, came with the king and force-fed me something slimy and tasteless, followed by a spoonful of some acrid, sticky liquid. Medicine, maybe. Maybe they were giving me something the king took before he had my magic.

I'm not sure why they bothered for the little good it had done him, but it seemed the king was desperate to keep me alive as long as possible.

I couldn't see, couldn't move. My every muscle strained and curled, withered on aching bones. Gums and tongue were swollen with sores. Blood dribbled from my mouth and stained the pillow. My chest shivered in endless convulsions. I was no longer bound or gagged. There was no need for it when I couldn't control my own body.

Othon was a big man, far larger than me, so everything I took from him was distilled, compressed down into me, filling me until it felt as though I would burst at the seams. And this would be the rest of my existence, taking this torture day by day, endlessly. Alone in darkness. Until I died.

Some days I wished their efforts to preserve me failed. I wished that I could be put out of my misery and just fade into the darkness that surrounded me.

But then I would think of Ara.

I hadn't heard her voice or felt her presence again. I longed for her to be close by me, as though her very closeness could revive me, make me well and whole.

During one visit, Othon had mocked her efforts, still out searching for me. But what had been meant to taunt me only gave me strength. It fed my hope and allowed me to dream that maybe, one day, I would get away from this suffering. Ara hadn't stopped looking. She still thought of me, too. As wretched as I was, there was somebody, even one person, who cared enough to try to find me.

And when all I could do was curl up and cry in blinding agony, I would cling to my sanity by dreaming of her.

I dreamed we'd stayed together in that room on the night of the first ball, hiding from my stepsisters, eating cake and sharing stories. That I hadn't run from her, that I'd stayed to feel the touch of her fingers on my waist for longer.

I dreamed when we met a second time that we didn't leave the storeroom to warn the king, that we stayed in that aisle between barrels, pressed together in the dark, my lips at her neck.

I dreamed we danced, and danced the last time we were together, and Prince Creston never interrupted, and there was no blood, no injury, no sickness. No pain.

And I dreamed that she saved me. Every time the secret door swung open and the light of a lantern burned my eyes, I would dream it was her kneeling before me, pulling me into her arms, and reviving me with a kiss.

But it was only ever a dream.

In reality, I flopped in a stupor, being spoon-fed sludge to keep my body alive, and then every time, afterwards, the door would lock again. Time lurched and slipped like molasses as I was pressed ever smaller under the heavy weight of pain.

I would heal the king. I would be fed and tended. I would dream. I would be saved. I would still be in the cell. Ara came to me, sword in one hand, the other at my cheek, her face a dreamlike blur.

"Ellasyn, please live," she would whisper. Arms would wrap around me, under me, and lift me up. She held me cradled, as though I was as weightless as a broken doll.

She carried me out of the cell.

My cheek pressed against the black velvet of her guard uniform, and I stared up at her face, my vision clearing enough to see the angry set to her jaw. For some reason, it made me cry.

I clung to her without strength and waited to wake again. Alone. Waited for the dream to be over and for my endless torture to repeat again.

But the dream shifted, and we moved in darkness down empty corridors as though flying. Ara's arms felt warm and so real. My mind regained just enough focus to become confused.

My voice was a crackling whisper. "Am I still dreaming?"

"My heart, no. Stay with me. Stay awake."

This made me cry harder. Still unbelieving. Still waiting to be back in my cell.

Ara slammed to a stop, ducked to the side, and waited for someone to pass as she squeezed me close, shushing my tears, then we moved again.

It couldn't be real. "How did you find me?"

Ara pushed through a door, then lay me onto a bed. She hastened back to lock the door. Was this her chamber? It was too dark to see. A soft-edged blob of white light came from my left, and I squinted against the glow. The moon, through a window. Gone too when Ara swished the curtains closed.

"I searched and searched the city. I worried I would never find you, until I spoke with a baker." She returned to my side, pressed a hand to my cheek again, then felt my forehead. "A baker whose daughter swore she'd been run over by a carriage and then miraculously healed when 'the mad servant lady with the burns' touched her."

Ara moved away, and I whimpered, longing to feel her touch again, as though it had healing magic too. I wanted to plead with her to come back, then porcelain clinked, and she returned, dabbing my face with a damp cloth. The still-healing cut on my cheek stung.

"That's how I found where you lived. Then I met your stepsister, who told me your full name and that you'd saved her from a fate worse than death, but her father had sold you to the king."

"Audred?" I sobbed her name.

"Then *Tobin*—" Ara muttered a curse under her breath. "—told me of the secret chamber the king had taken you to. He hadn't realized who you were until I started asking about the woman handed over to the king, but once he realized, he wanted to help you, as you helped comfort him after his 'close call.' He said he would have sooner but hadn't recognized you as the same woman from the ball. Which … honestly … Men!"

I shied then, turning away from the cloth Ara wiped my face with. "I must look so awful compared to how you knew me."

Ara took my chin in her hand and gentled me back toward her. She leaned in and pressed her lips to my forehead. "You are you. And I would not have it any other way."

A shiver ran up my spine. I shook my head weakly, still feeling this was a trap, a dream. It couldn't be real. "But the key. The king has the only key."

Ara moved from the bed and searched through a wardrobe. "I'd worked out by then that you had some kind of healing magic. I'm a genius, I know. But I also worked out its cost. I remembered Tobin's shoulder, strangely unmarred, and how blood had run down yours. I remembered your burns from the explosion you weren't near. So, I asked the fire-breather for help. He didn't hesitate to return the gift you'd given him, even if it meant using his fine illusion skills to pick the king's pockets."

She returned with something in one hand, then reached for the buttons of my soiled servant uniform. "May I?"

I nodded, too overwhelmed to speak. She carefully stripped the filthy outer layer off me and violently flung it away across the room. As she helped me into a gown of thick, soft wool, my body almost felt alive again, warmth returning to my chest.

I leaned into her as she fastened the final button. "You saved me."

She stepped back, holding me in her gaze, and shook her head fiercely. "No, El, I didn't."

She didn't. She didn't save me. The spell felt shattered, the dream ready to crumble. I held my breath, waiting to wake up.

"You saved *yourself.*" Her voice rung with passion. "It was you, your acts of kindness being repaid, that saved you. Every pain you selflessly took from another became a marker on my map to finding you. If you weren't the incredible, kind-hearted person you are, you would still be in that cell."

My arms shot out for Ara as though I was a drowning child in stormy waves, and I wept. She drew me in and tucked me under her chin, tight to her soft chest. I clung to her, wracked by emotion, tears washing away all doubt that this was real. This was *real.* She came for me, and I was saved, and I couldn't slow the fall of saltwater for how that filled my heart to bursting.

Then, a clock chimed.

My sobbing stilled and silenced in an instant as a chill fell over me. "What's the time?"

"Late. I waited till the cover of night to retrieve you. Probably midnight."

I shot back, wide-eyed. "The king will be coming for me. He always does, every day, after twelve chimes, with a lantern, always at midnight. He'll find me gone at any moment."

Ara grunted. "I thought we'd have more time, at least some more hours of darkness to decide on our plan and make our escape."

She looked about wildly for a moment before her attention snapped back to me. "Every day? He inflicted this on you *every day?*" Her words dripped with fury.

She rose to her feet and started pacing, then hissed in a low whisper, "He has been looking so well lately, and at first, I was happy to see my father feeling better. Until I worked out *how* he was feeling better. I can't ever forgive him for what he's done to you. Someday, I will confront him for this, mark me, but first, I must make sure you are safe from him.

We have to leave."

As renewed as I had become in Ara's presence, a heaviness settled into my gut. What cost would saving me, avenging me, have for her? One that was too great. "I heard your brother. I heard you both talking when he said he would leave."

"You were that close?" Ara's voice held so much anguish that I was glad I couldn't see her expression in the dim light. It may have broken me completely.

I shook my head. "You can't confront the king. You can't let him know you've helped me. With Creston leaving, it is your entire kingdom at stake, your chance to rule it the way you've always dreamed. I can make my own way from here—run away and disappear. They may think I escaped on my own. You needn't sacrifice anything for me."

Ara threw her hands into the air. "How? How could you not wish revenge for what has been done to you?"

"I'm well acquainted with how much pain there is in the world. Why would I want to be the cause of more?"

Ara's pacing stalled for a long moment, her head hung.

"Ara, don't worry for me. This kingdom could be yours."

She turned to me, teeth glinting in a smile as she reached for my hands. "How could I be worthy of this kingdom if I gave you up to receive it? What kind of ruler would I be if I didn't have my heart?"

She tugged at my fingers, pulling me up to stand before

her. I was amazed my body could hold itself up, that my heart, now hers, could beat so strong. All that strength, I owed to her. Her expression was resolved, and I couldn't deny her.

"Then we must run," I said.

Ara nodded. "We flee together. We'll find our way. If my halfwit brother can, so can we. But first, I left something with your sister that I want to collect."

"At my home? Trolaine may be there. It will be dangerous."

Ara huffed. "The man who has been abusing you for so long, who would sell you like a bushel of wheat? I won't let him harm you again. And as much as I'd like to slice his rump from his bones and hand it to him roasted on a plate, I'll save that for another time. We will be fast, and then we will be free."

Ara scooped me up again, carrying me through the quiet nighttime castle.

We reached the stables and stole a horse. As we rode across moonlit fields, I wondered, where would we go? Where would be safe? It felt like nowhere could shelter us from the king's wrath. I had no uncertainty that he would hunt me to the ends of the earth. We would have to go to the ends of the earth and beyond.

In all the years I'd considered running from Trolaine, I'd always been too scared of what might be out there in the world, beyond this city, this kingdom. It looked like now I would find out. And I was so grateful that I wouldn't be alone.

I leaned into Ara's back, drawing on her warmth in the cool night air, and thought of all she would be giving up for me. It didn't seem right.

I considered facing Trolaine again, or my stepsisters. Returning home, even for the briefest time, scared me. I had nothing to pack, nothing I owned. But if I was leaving forever, it would be nice to say goodbye to my family home, one final time.

FIFTEEN

ARA REFUSED TO tell me what she had left with my stepsister. I couldn't imagine what was worth the risk of returning for and suggested a few times that we didn't, but Ara held fast to her mission.

She kept the horse moving at a gentle canter, taking us down narrow paths between stone-walled fields and through thin pine forests under the starry sky. She had pushed to a gallop once, but my nose started bleeding, and she'd had to hold me from falling off the horse as I coughed. Ara kept us moving forward, craning her neck often to check on me and scan behind us for any followers.

I directed her through to the bottom of our property, and when we reached the orchard, Ara slid gracefully down to the ground to open the gate, then led the horse and me through.

We moved slowly, quietly, through the thin trees. When the fallen treasure tree came into view, my heart lurched at the memory of my stepfather's brutal actions. A reminder of why we were running from this kingdom.

I cleared my throat. "Can you take me closer to the gravestones so I can say goodbye?"

Ara nodded, remaining silent and watchful as she took in the strange scenery. Mice, sparrows, and rabbits scattered as we drew closer. They ran in all directions, some straight toward me before seeming to think better of being close to the horse's hooves.

"This is—this was—the tree that gifted me my gowns," I told Ara.

"That was real? You truly weren't lying when you said a tree gave you your dress. And there I was thinking you were trying to gain my interest by being contrary and mysterious. Which, to be honest, completely worked."

Ara led me over to between my parent's graves. Pieces of pottery and metal clattered softly under the horse's hooves. "I wish you could have seen it before it was destroyed. Every little treasure that built it up was a gift from a creature I saved. It was so spellbinding, even before it showed the full extent of its magic."

"Perhaps when we find a new home, you can rebuild such

a thing again, one act of kindness at a time."

I smiled softly but felt in my heart that it wasn't my kindness that had built the tree, or at least, not that alone. Otherwise, why here? Why right over my mother's grave? Wherever I ended up next, I would be far away from this magic, and that made me deeply sad.

"I would prefer to hope that in my new home, there wouldn't be so many acts of cruelty to be reversed in the first place."

I closed my eyes, feeling bashful in front of Ara, but I needed to do this. "Thank you," I said to the tree, to the animals, to the poor clockwork horse, to my mother, to any magic of the world that might listen. "Goodbye, Mamma. Goodbye, Pa. Goodbye, Grandmamma. I love you."

I had so much I wished to say but kept it brief, knowing every moment here was a risk.

The sky still cloaked us in darkness with no sign yet of the rising sun. Ara started the horse moving again and walked close by my leg as she took us to the house.

At the back door to the manor, Ara reached up to lift me from the saddle.

With my feet on the ground, I took a deep breath. It rattled in my chest. But I could see clearly and had enough control again over my limbs that I didn't simply melt onto the dirt. "I think I can walk now. At least a little."

Ara kept her hands around each side of my ribcage and tilted her head when I wobbled. But she didn't argue. "I'm with you."

The dress she'd given me swam about my shorter figure, and I had to lift it to avoid stepping on the hem as I walked over the paved courtyard that led to the back of the house. The finely woven wool was soft under my fingers and almost white, except where my bleeding nose had marred it with a few rose-petal-shaped drops.

I pointed up to a window with a shaking finger. "That's Audred's bedroom."

Ara scooped up a handful of pea-sized rocks and threw them one at a time at the glass, making soft plinking sounds in the quiet night. After the fourth stone hit the pane, the curtains shifted, and a pale face peered down, then disappeared again.

Moments later, a tiny, warm light flickered through the kitchen window. There was a click, and the heavy door swung with a creak. Two faces now peered out at us—Audred holding a candle, with Asterra clinging close, watching over her shoulder.

They wore matching blue nightgowns, which rustled in the soft breeze. "Cinders?"

I approached up the back steps, almost tripping on weak and wobbly legs. Ara caught me around the elbow and kept me steady. Within the small pool of candlelight, my stepsisters stared, wide-eyed. Then Audred's face cracked and crumpled with emotion.

"Oh, look at you. Look at you!" She stared mostly at the slice marking my cheek. "I can't believe Father did it, that he sold you away! I didn't believe at all when he said you'd tried to hurt someone. I know you would never do something like that. And I don't want to marry a prince if it is at the price of losing a sister."

To her side, Asterra shook her head with a wild, nervous energy.

My lips trembled and the backs of my eyes burned with tears. How could I leave them here with their cruel father? Would they come with us if I asked? A low creak from above us made me jump. The wind blew, and a shutter rattled.

Ara put a hand on Audred's shoulder. "What I left with you, will you fetch it? We cannot stay."

Audred nodded and gestured for us to come inside. She lit another candle on the table with the flame from her own.

We waited close by the open door as Audred turned away, then back again, eyebrows drawn and crooked, lit from below with the candle she sheltered close to her chest. "Where will you go?" Her voice quavered.

I opened my mouth with no answer to her question, only wanting to ask in return if she would come with us, and then there was another sound behind us.

In the corner of my eye, something swung, glinting in the moonlight. Ara gasped and sidestepped. Metal ripped through cloth. And Ara screamed.

The cry cut off quickly, and she grabbed for me, pushing me further inside. We tumbled in beside the hearth that glowed with only a few hot coals.

Ara drew her sword and turned to face who had struck her from behind.

My eyes landed on Trolaine holding the same axe he'd felled my tree with, and I watched in horror as he raised it to swing at the princess again. Ara lifted her sword as a warning. Her other arm hung limp, and her fingers shook as blood ran down them, dripping onto the floor.

"What have you done?" he yelled at me. "You and this— who is this guard? You traitors!"

"She is a princess, and you've hurt her!" I snapped back. From slightly behind her, I could see where the axe had gone through the padding of her uniform across the top of her arm.

Trolaine seemed horrified, but only for the briefest moment. "It doesn't matter. I had a deal with *the king.* And you have ruined everything. I won't let my deal be broken by you, or anyone."

He stepped forward, and Ara laughed free and loud in a way that caught him on the spot.

"You don't know?" she chuckled.

"Know what?" he grunted, shifting his hold on the axe.

"Oh no. Now I feel like a jerk telling you that your little princely prize ran away days ago."

"What?"

Ara smirked. "Prince Creston. He's gone. There's no more deal to be had."

Audred gasped and put her hands over her mouth. Her eyes shimmered with tears. Asterra took the candle from her other hand and put it down on the table before she could drop it.

Trolaine scoffed. "You're lying. The king hasn't said—"

"The king doesn't care about you, or Creston, or his marriage, or your daughter, or *anybody* but himself." Ara's voice changed, so low and venomous that Trolaine's disbelief seemed to burn away in the face of it.

He pointed his axe at Audred, shaking it as he yelled. "You didn't try hard enough. I did all of this for you, and you couldn't make yourself good enough for the prince to want you. He would rather leave his *throne* than be with you! What have I done to be cursed with such useless daughters?"

Audred shuddered, tears streaming as her legs gave way beneath her. Trolaine marched, snarling, toward her. Asterra clung at her sister's side, trying to draw her back to her feet.

"Stop it!" I shouted, stumbling to place myself in his path, to block him from my sisters. "Leave them alone."

With a roar of spittle, Trolaine raised his axe over his

head. It came down and clashed against steel. Ara's sword swept up the handle of the axe, catching at the head, swinging it out and away from her, but he held onto it fast.

Two pairs of hands also grabbed me from behind, pulling me back with them, pressing me between Dred and Terra.

Trolaine turned on Ara, lashing the axe out in a wild arc. She raised her sword straight in front of her chest and neatly leaned away from the sharp edge of his attack.

Trolaine overextended, the momentum of the axe swinging him in a circle, but Ara remained still.

He continued around in his circle, growling in fury, and punched the axe out, trying to hammer Ara with the blunt end. She slapped it away with the flat of her sword. Concentration and something else gleamed in her eyes.

Even though Ara only had one working arm, she was fighting like a master warrior, and Trolaine couldn't touch her.

"Drop your weapon. I don't wish to down you in front of your daughters." Ara ducked a swing aimed for her head. "But if you ruin my hair, so help me …"

Trolaine didn't listen. He turned toward me and his daughters and lunged. But as Ara stepped to maneuver him away from us, he grinned and changed direction, charging her, throwing his whole body at Ara before she could bring her sword between them.

She smacked back into the wall on her injured side and

hissed through gritted teeth. Her face lightened a few shades, and her eyes rolled to whites, eyelashes fluttering.

Trolaine stepped back to raise his axe high.

"Ara!"

Her eyes snapped back open as the axe came down.

A flurry of movement filled the kitchen. Asterra shrieked. Tiny furry and feathered forms flooded in through the open door, rushing about underfoot. Rats, mice, rabbits, pigeons, owls, and sparrows flocked through the room like a hurricane.

Trolaine tripped away from them. The axe faltered, plunged into a wooden beam beside Ara's neck, and stuck fast. Trolaine gritted his teeth as he tried to tug it free.

She raised a booted foot and kicked out, catching Trolaine square in the chest.

He sailed backward and landed hard in the hot ashes of the hearth, red sparks flying from the remaining embers. He rolled about, howling, as his clothes singed and smoked, and tumbled out onto the floor in a puff of gray soot.

The fluttering and skittering menagerie cleared, the animals disappearing again. My heart also felt as though it fluttered and skittered along with them. All these lives acting for me, putting themselves at risk for me, making sacrifices for me, caused my pulse to beat with the question, *Why me, why me?*

And the warmth in my chest answered, *Because I am loved.*

"Ropes!" Ara ordered, and dropped herself beside Trolaine,

rolling him over and wrenching his arms behind his back as he tried to wriggle away. She held him fast, her stoic expression never hinting at the pain she must be in.

I pulled a drawer open, took a bundle of roasting twine, and handed it to Ara. She wrapped it around Trolaine's wrists multiple times until it was secure. Her fingers shook, and the twine and Trolaine's hands ended up stained in her blood as she worked.

She moved to bind his feet as well. A sheen of perspiration glittered over her dark forehead. She wiped it away with the cuff of her sleeve.

I knelt beside her and reached for her hand. "I can fix the injury for you."

She twitched away from me, a frown on her beautiful features. "Don't you even dare."

I backed away, stung by her rejection. For a brief flash, I saw my mother, her body broken, also telling me no. My voice was small, lacking determination. "I … I made a vow. I can't stand by and see you hurt when I can help. Please, let me help you. I can endure it."

Shaking her head at me, Ara touched her fingers lightly to my cheek. "Why? Why must you be the keeper of every agony? Just because you can endure it doesn't mean you must. You don't owe that to me or anyone else. You've already taken on too much pain. I can handle this."

A WISH OF ASHES AND GLASS

I leaned into her touch, my chest swelling with a warm rush of emotion as though it could burst, and it felt as though something did break inside of me. Like a bone being reset, a sharp break of something long ago twisted the wrong way, being righted.

I had taken on so much suffering throughout the years, as though I deserved it, as though I owed the use of my body and magic to all. As though I was always trying to pay a debt that was never truly mine, backed up by the vow of a grieving child.

I had already broken that vow when I defied the king the first time, and it had felt right. The awakening truth that the gift of my magic should be granted not from obligation, but by choice, bloomed in my heart like springtime.

Trolaine strained against the bonds holding him, writhing like a trussed-up hog. "You'll all be hung for this, you—"

Ara jammed a handful of filthy lilac rag squares into his mouth. "Damn, I sort of wish I'd had an apple. We could have got the fire going again, had a nice roast."

Audred and Asterra remained clung together, staring with dinner-plate eyes.

"I'm kidding." Ara laughed, then in sotto voce said, "Mostly."

I looked from Trolaine to them and back again. "What happens now?"

Ara shrugged, then winced, regret on her face. "I would take him in to be imprisoned for all his cruelty and crimes, but unfortunately, I don't think I have that authority anymore, what with the slight treason I've been doing in stealing you away from the king." She looked at me with a sweet smile. "So, we should probably keep moving right away."

I stood back up. My eyes kept turning from Trolaine to my sisters, over and over. "But what happens now for them?"

Ara worked on the final knots of Trolaine's bindings, fixing him to the leg of the table. "Huh. I suppose he can't stay tied up forever, as much as he deserves it. If everyone turns around and doesn't watch, I could run him through real quick and—Kidding! Mostly."

"I can't leave them here with him. He will punish them for this, even if we're gone. And if he is found murdered, I doubt they will fare much better." I turned to Audred. "Come with us, please. I don't know where we will go, but we will be together. You'll be away from him."

My sister stared back, unblinking and statue-like. Asterra tugged on her dress, nodding, which seemed to wake Audred from her daze. Her gaze turned to her father grunting and twitching against his bonds, still attempting to free himself. Then she nodded too.

Ara looked up at me from her crouched position. "Are you sure? We've already been here too long. We only have one horse. Taking them with us is a risk."

"I don't want to leave them here. I *can't* leave them here."

Ara held my gaze for a moment, then nodded. She barked at the others. "Go and pack. Fast. One change of clothing. One thing you own that's worth the most that we can hawk along the way. And Audred, what I left with you, please."

My sisters nodded and left. I grabbed a sack, filling it with any food, tools, and other essentials I could reach in the kitchen.

Ara groaned as she stood back up.

Abandoning my task, I moved beside her. "I can at least bandage the wound for you while the others pack."

Ara nodded and stripped off her guard jacket and the white shirt beneath, leaving her in a sleeveless undershirt. My cheeks flamed at how the thin cotton clung to her glistening chest. Keeping on task, I gathered some muslin strips and a jar of ointment. Blood painted stickily down the length of her arm.

She sat on a wooden stool, and I carefully dabbed the pungent gel onto the gash.

Ara watched me work. "You're doing the right thing for your sisters. Getting them away from that man will be good for them. But are you sure it is worth it?"

I didn't hesitate. "They haven't always been good to me, but I can't leave them to suffer. They are my sisters."

Ara smiled softly as I wrapped her arm. "I get it. Look, you must realize I know how complicated sister relationships can be more than anyone."

My fingers froze in their task, and I swallowed hard. "You don't have to leave them behind for me."

Deep creases formed across Ara's forehead. Her tight bun had come loose, and an unwinding braid swished on her shoulders as she shook her head. "I need to get you somewhere safe. Then I can return, try to … I don't know. I don't know."

Tears filled my eyes, and I tried to wipe them with my shoulder as I finished securing Ara's bandage. She reached for me, brushing a hand along my cheek, careful of the cut there, then wrapped her fingers up behind my head, tangling them into my hair. She pulled me closer, gently, her eyes hooded.

"But what I do know is that your heart holds such kindness that it draws me in like an arrow to a bullseye, and I would do anything for you."

I half smiled. "I know. You drew a sword on the prince for me. You were ready to spit-roast my stepfather for me."

He grunted again from behind the table.

"Still willing." Ara smirked.

"Please don't," I whispered, cheeks flushing hot at her touch. "Otherwise, I may kiss you so forcefully in my gratitude that you won't think me sweet and kind anymore."

Ara pulled me closer. "All right, that's it. Let's get married this instant."

Asterra ran back into the room, panting, a stuffed bag under one arm and her cheeks bright pink. Ara and I broke apart.

Audred arrived a moment later with her excuse. "I packed a few things for you, too. Since you didn't have your own."

She came over beside us and handed Ara something wrapped in black silk. "And this."

"It's for El, actually." Ara tugged at the cloth, undoing the knot that held it closed.

Before I could see what lay beneath, the room became brighter. A flickering, warm light spilled in to overtake the tiny glow of the two candles.

"It can't already be dawn," I muttered, turning to the open back door.

Out in the night, a cloud of dotted flames floated in the darkness. Torches, dozens of them, hundreds, held by soldiers, a thick crowd of them ringing around the building.

A voice boomed out, "Surrender yourselves! On the king's orders."

Sixteen

ARA STOOD IN her sleeveless undershirt, sword readied, the white bandage on her arm stark against her dark skin in the moonlight. I stood with her, my hand in hers, facing an army of soldiers and the king himself.

Beside Ara, I grew strong, as though the way she made me feel was a fire flaring through me, burning all the sickness I had taken on away.

Across from us in the paved courtyard, the king looked as equally diminished as I had been renewed. His hunched back and hacking cough showed the cost of missing his midnight treatment.

"Father dearest, what brings you here?" Ara asked slyly. "You shouldn't be out this late. It can't be good for your illness."

Between the torches surrounding him, Othon's skin shimmered with sweat. He straightened up and cried, "Don't play games! You have done this to me. Give me back my cure now, and I might spare you."

The horse we had stolen spooked at the yelling, dancing on the spot and pulling against the post where it had been tied.

We'd sent Audred and Asterra through the house to flee out the front, but they returned behind us and whispered, "They are all around. There's no way through."

Ara's nose twitched at their news, but she didn't take her eyes off the king. "She's not your *cure*. I won't hand her over to that fate."

Othon gestured to the troops backing him. "You're smarter than this, Miara. You've no way to stop me."

"Maybe not, but that doesn't mean I have to help you. I'm done with that, helping you use others' lives for your own gain, spending them as though they are worth nothing. How many of my soldiers have gone to their deaths on your orders? All those who have fought and suffered without you ever knowing their names or faces. But I know. I knew them all and have wept for every single one of them. Still, I followed your orders." She breathed out, long and heavy. "No more."

Othon chuckled without humor. "You think I would ever let *you* command my armies again? You are for the rope, my daughter. You will hang as all the traitors around me have this night."

A WISH OF ASHES AND GLASS

Ara's hand clenched in mine. "Whose life have you taken now, Father?"

"Your accomplice in this plot. Hareth is gone and can't help you anymore."

"Hareth? He didn't do a thing."

"He was one of few who knew where the girl was kept and the only one I shared the key with. Of course he helped you."

Ara shook her head, smiling grimly. "That's not how I got the key. You've killed the person most loyal to you. As you would kill anyone loyal to you if it served you."

"Liar!"

Ara brought her sword up slowly. "I truly don't care if you believe me. I know my path now, and I am ready to follow my heart. I should always have been strong enough to do so. If I had, maybe I could have saved more lives from you and your greed. Now, I know my life has no value to you. But I will fight to the last to defend the life of this woman you do value, to keep her from your misuse."

King Othon grunted. "Enough of this. Guards, take them. No harm to the blond thing. End the others."

Audred and Asterra whimpered, hiding behind the kitchen doorframe. Ara dropped my hand, moving into a fighting stance.

Guards shuffled—shoulders shifted, feet repositioned, and looks were shared side to side amidst the flaming glow of torchlight. But nobody drew their weapons. Not one of

the soldiers approached.

"What is this mutiny? I have ordered you!" Othon cried, voice rattling. Red spatter marred his blue-tinted lips.

Tobin moved first, raising a fist and thumping it to his chest as though in salute. He nodded to Ara. The guards at his side followed, and soon, every soldier stood in that pose, facing their princess.

Ara nodded once and lowered her blade.

With a wail, Othon snatched a sword from the belt of the nearest guard and crossed the courtyard in three long strides.

I stepped between him and Ara, and the sword point stilled near my neck. "You can't kill me," I said, staring down the length of the trembling blade and into Othon's eyes. "There will be no one to heal you if I am dead."

He breathed heavily, chest groaning up and down. "And if you don't heal me, I will be dead. Everyone here seems determined for that outcome, so I will take as many of you with me as I can!"

Ara reached for me from behind, but I held up a hand, warding her off. I lowered my voice, speaking just to Othon. "Don't. Please. Don't choose this. You don't have long to live. You could choose to spend it with your family. You could spend your remaining time with love around you. Your children will forgive you. Please choose differently and let them."

A WISH OF ASHES AND GLASS

His arm dropped, not seemingly from any conscious action, but as though the effort to hold the weapon was too much for him to sustain. The sword tip wobbled, trailing and poking down my front, from neck to sternum, too weak to break the skin.

Othon loosed a long moan, then shook his head and growled at me. "Don't speak of choice to me. You choosing not to heal me is killing me! It is murder! Heal me. I am your king!"

I lifted my hands, staring at my open palms, before curling my fingers closed and bringing them back to my sides. "You are my king. But my body is my own. And I won't let you take that from me. I would not give you my health when you cannot even give your own family love. Living for the sake of living is worth nothing without love."

Othon's face twisted into a monstrous mask. His eyes bulged. Red froth foamed near his lips.

He screamed in staccato, "AH AH AAAH," as he raised the sword up over his head.

It came clattering down, out of his hands, onto the stones between us. Then his body fell on top of it, face down with a crunch.

Ara pushed past me, rushing to kneel at his side. She turned his head, shaking him, pressing fingers to his neck, before shooting back to her feet abruptly and unsteadily.

"He's dead," she whispered, then pressed herself into my arms. Her body rocked with silent sobs. I brought my hands up around her, pulling her in tight.

"I'm sorry. I'm so sorry," I mumbled into her hair.

"It's not your fault."

My body shook too, whether from her grief or my own couldn't be distinguished. "But I could have … Maybe I should have …"

"No. You owed him nothing. My heart, only you would regret not suffering to save such a man. But now he is gone … I don't know what to do. What does our kingdom do?"

Outside of our embrace, there was an echoing rustle of movement. We pulled apart warily to see every guard on their knees.

It was Tobin who called into the night, "The king is dead! Long live the queen!"

I stepped back, dropping myself to my knees as well, and looked up at Ara haloed by the moon. "Under your rule, our kingdom will thrive."

SEVENTEEN

ARA WORE A black velvet gown with golden cuirass and epaulettes for her coronation.

The outfit perfectly displayed both her femininity and her immense strength. The heavier ceremonial pieces of her outfit had been shed as the celebration stretched on into the night, but the slim ring of her crown remained.

I smiled to see it resting on her forehead. A symbol of all that she had lost, but everything the kingdom had to gain. It suited her. My dress, all in shimmering gold with black lace accents over my shoulders, was designed to match hers in reverse. It was almost as fine as the gowns the treasure tree had gifted me. Almost.

Ara sighed on her throne and relaxed as the final well-wisher in the queue walked away to join in the revelry before us.

Nearby, Terra giggled louder than I'd ever heard her raise her little voice. She danced with Tobin, who had what seemed to be a fork lodged into his rump.

Ara had been entirely correct about his ability for improbable self-harm. Terra tried to draw him off the dance floor, but he shook his head, smiling as he yanked the fork free, and dragged her back his way, setting off more giggles again.

From my seat beside Ara, I sought Dred then, casting my eyes around the glittering ballroom and joyous dancers. I found her in the same place she'd remained all evening, by herself on a lounge in the corner.

I'd watched her politely refuse a number of advances already tonight, and I frowned to see her still alone. Terra and our family home had been left in Audred's stewardship, and she was trying so hard to get their lives back on track. On her face though, was a look of peace.

She'd come to me earlier in the day and hugged me tight. She told me that since her father had been imprisoned, she'd finally learned how to breathe.

"Checking on them again?" Ara teased with a smile.

I shrugged bashfully. "Only as often as you're checking on your sisters."

They were easy to spot, spinning about in the dancing crowd in their extravagantly bejeweled gowns. "Well, some

are still rather upset at losing Father, but Deeny, Meeny, Mornee, and Anne are—"

"Oh, stop! I *have* learned all their names now, I swear!" I blushed red at the memory of some of my early interactions with them all. Luckily, I'd found they were mostly as good humored as Queen Miara. Still Ara to me.

Prince Creston didn't return, but a missive had arrived to let Ara know he'd heard of their father's passing and would visit sometime to abdicate officially.

Ara had stared at the letter in shock for minutes before muttering, "I honestly thought he didn't have the stones for life outside the palace. I guess sometimes I can be wrong."

Turning in her throne, Ara faced me fully and pulled a parcel of black silk from a deep pocket of her gown. She held it out to me with a bow of her head. "I have something for you."

I took it, bewildered. "This is your coronation. Why do I get a gift?"

"You were meant to have it much sooner, but things have been a bit hectic." Ara gestured to her crown and everything around us.

I recognized the parcel as the one Ara had tried to give me on the night her father died. The silk was soft beneath my touch as I loosened the knot that tied the ends of the cloth, and the fabric slipped down, revealing a sparking glass slipper.

"What? How?"

"This is what I asked Audred to keep for me."

I ran my fingers over the cool, slick surface, marveling at the rainbows held within the glass. "I mean, how could it have lasted beyond midnight?"

"It wasn't meant to?"

"Everything else vanished once the clock chimed its twelfth stroke."

Ara nodded sadly. "I had shown the slipper to Audred during my search for you, to prove who I was looking for. But she said it couldn't possibly have been yours. That you owned nothing. But she had seen you at the third ball and felt your magic, so we knew there must be something more that we didn't understand. I asked Audred to keep this safe, in case my rescue mission went awry."

I smirked. "I'm shocked you doubted yourself."

"I know, out of character, but it was my first time stealing a whole entire woman from the king himself. I thought some caution was warranted."

I smiled and teared up at the same time.

Ara reached across and placed a hand over mine on the slipper. "Once I learned about your magical tree, its origin and destruction, it seemed even more important that you had this. That you had one tangible reminder of that magic."

I pulled both the slipper and Ara's hand up to my chest,

pressing them to my heart as though I could merge them into me forever.

"Thank you," I whispered, my voice hushed with emotion. "But this is my second reminder of that magic. My first is you."

Ara leaned in and kissed me on the temple. "Always have to one-up me on the sweetness, don't you?"

Taking a few deep breaths, I wiped my eyes, and my smile grew.

"Actually, I have something for you, too." I reached down beside my seat and pulled up a plate I had put aside. "Although it isn't nearly as—"

"Oh yes! Oh, you amazing woman." Ara snatched the plate of petite brown cakes from my fingers and grinned as she stuffed one into her mouth. "When are we getting married again?"

"I love you, too."

I laughed freely as she stood up and reached for me. "Come on, let's dance."

The guests parted for us as we strode together onto the floor.

As we clasped each other in a waltzing embrace, I kept thinking of the magic of that glass slipper and decided to share with Ara the secrets my mother had shared with me, that the women in our family had kept for generations.

"My great-grandmother was blessed by a faery, and that

blessing has passed down through the women in her line, each of us with a different magical gift. Great-Grandmother could cheat death, but then that fate would befall someone else. She died young."

Ara watched me with sparkling golden eyes and let me continue.

"Then Grandmamma, she wept diamond tears but only when those she loved suffered. So, she made sure her family were always happy. And I believe in my heart that Mamma had a gift that helped me from the grave. That she had the power to help me when I needed it the most but would never be able to see the outcome herself."

"Typical fae trickery. They hardly sound like gifts at all," Ara muttered.

Our gowns swished against each other, and my sigh matched their sound. "But they have been. They taught kindness, which is a gift in itself."

"I suppose so. What tyrants they could have been, your grand and great-grandmothers, with those powers. But they chose to risk themselves, chose to forfeit the riches of their gifts, and chose love instead. What a world we'd know if all chose kindness that way." Ara's voice was thick and low, the glitter of tears along her eyelids. "With such kindness is how I intend to live my life. That is how I hope to lead our people."

"And you will, because you love them." In the weeks

since the king's passing, I had seen how Ara had managed her soldiers, knowing every one of them by name. How she continued to act with logic tempered by compassion. I was so proud of her, so full of hope for the future of our kingdom, I could hardly contain it.

Ara placed her lips on my temple. "I love you most of all. You, who heard me when no one else would listen, who saw me without the influence of my crown, who helped me without asking anything in return. You have my heart forever."

Old insecurities and fears burbled in my stomach under the weight of her perfect gaze. "Even with my scars?"

Ara brushed a finger over the slim, pink line down my cheek. "Your scars are a tapestry of all the good you have done in your life, all the kindness you've given. You are the most beautiful person I've ever seen."

I was glad she found them beautiful because their number continued to grow. "And it's your love that has given me the power to give my kindness freely."

"My love and the love of our entire kingdom."

It had taken me a while to work it out. After the tree had been destroyed, my injuries and the illness I had taken from the king all healed far faster than normal. I had credited it to the magic of the tree while it still existed, so how did its magic still affect me once it was gone?

Soon, I realized it had never been the tree that healed

me. It was the magic of love.

It was Ara's care for me that sped my healing after each ball, and she loved me now so deeply I could continue my vow to heal all who came to me for aid.

And the more I was loved, the faster I healed. And the more people I healed, the more I was loved.

The broken finger I'd taken from a child that morning had already repaired itself, yet Ara pulled my knuckles to her lips and kissed them.

"As fast as you heal now, I still don't like seeing you hurt."

"I can endure anything, my queen, with you by my side to kiss it all better."

In the distance, a clock chimed midnight. And we kept dancing.

NEED MORE HAPPILY EVER AFTERS?

When Zari discovers that a billionaire is enslaving people who are gifted with magic, she takes her little sister's place as his captive. But with no powers of her own, how long can she survive the cruel tests and tasks?

In this modern day, urban fantasy retelling of Rumpelstiltskin, can a young woman escape a cage of gold and lies?

ABOUT THE AUTHOR

WHETHER IT'S PAINTING artworks or writing novels, creating fantasy works is Selina's biggest passion. She lives in Australia with her husband and daughter and loves food, gardening, geekery, and all things fantasy.

FIND OUT MORE
ABOUT SELINA

Official Website www.selinafenech.com

Memory's Wake Trilogy

A modern girl lost in and hunted in a fairy tale world. An illustrated young adult portal fantasy with Arthurian and Victorian themes.

Empath Chronicles

Teenagers with superpowers fueled by emotions … what could go wrong? A young adult superhero romance.

More Books by Selina A Fenech

Beshadowed

You have been lied to. Werewolves, vampires, ghosts … they aren't what you think. What is really lurking in the dark? A spooky urban fantasy.

Heartsblood

Her blood is irresistible, but is it worth the cost? A vampire romance for adults.